"Tracey, I Want You To Marry Me."

Grant's proposal staggered her. "I...um, I don't know what to say," Tracey replied. She'd always wanted marriage and children. Now it was being offered to her on a silver platter. Though not the conventional way of beginning of a family, she'd have the chance to raise two very special little girls.

Tracey couldn't love them more if they were her own flesh and blood. They were a part of Grant, whom she'd loved for most of her life. But he didn't need to know that, did he? He'd made it clear that he still thought of her as his best friend.

"Say yes. The girls need you. I need you, too," Grant said.

This was her chance for a fulfilling life, what she'd wanted, dreamed of for so long, Tracey thought. With just one small word, it could all be hers....

Dear Reader,

Welcome in the millennium, and the 20th anniversary of Silhouette, with Silhouette Desire—where you're guaranteed powerful, passionate and provocative love stories that feature rugged heroes and spirited heroines who experience the full emotional intensity of falling in love!

We are happy to announce that the ever-fabulous Annette Broadrick will give us the first MAN OF THE MONTH of the 21st century, *Tall, Dark & Texan.* A highly successful Texas tycoon opens his heart and home to a young woman who's holding a secret. Lindsay McKenna makes a dazzling return to Desire with *The Untamed Hunter,* part of her highly successful MORGAN'S MERCENARIES: THE HUNTERS miniseries. Watch sparks fly when a hard-bitten mercenary is reunited with a spirited doctor—the one woman who got away.

A Texan Comes Courting features another of THE KEEPERS OF TEXAS from Lass Small's miniseries. A cowboy discovers the woman of his dreams—and a shocking revelation. Alexandra Sellers proves a virginal heroine can bring a Casanova to his knees in *Occupation: Casanova.* Desire's themed series THE BRIDAL BID debuts with Amy J. Fetzer's *Going…Going…Wed!* And in *Conveniently His,* Shirley Rogers presents best friends turned lovers in a marriage-of-convenience story.

Each and every month, Silhouette Desire offers you six exhilarating journeys into the seductive world of romance. So start off the new millennium right, by making a commitment to sensual love and treating yourself to all six!

Enjoy!

Joan Marlow Golan
Senior Editor, Silhouette Desire

Please address questions and book requests to:
Silhouette Reader Service
U.S.: 3010 Walden Ave., P.O. Box 1325, Buffalo, NY 14269
Canadian: P.O. Box 609, Fort Erie, Ont. L2A 5X3

Conveniently His

SHIRLEY ROGERS

Silhouette®

Desire

Published by Silhouette Books

America's Publisher of Contemporary Romance

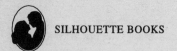 **SILHOUETTE BOOKS**

ISBN 0-373-76266-6

CONVENIENTLY HIS

This edition published by arrangement with Harlequin Books S.A.

® and TM are trademarks of Harlequin Books S.A., used under license. Trademarks indicated with ® are registered in the United States Patent and Trademark Office, the Canadian Trade Marks Office and in other countries.

Visit us at www.romance.net

Printed in U.S.A.

Books by Shirley Rogers

Silhouette Desire

Cowboys, Babies and Shotgun Vows #1176
Conveniently His #1266

SHIRLEY ROGERS

lives in the Hampton Roads area of Virginia, where she was born and raised. Being one of five children, she says, gives her lots of experience to draw on when writing her stories. She is happily married and the proud mother of a son and daughter. In her free time, she likes reading romances, traveling, seeing movies and shopping with her daughter.

Readers can write to Shirley at PMB #189, 1920-125 Centerville Tpke., Virginia Beach, VA 23464.

To my husband, Roger, for his continued
support and enthusiasm

One

"When are you going to marry me and put me out of my misery?" Grant Dennison asked without a trace of amusement as he watched his best friend clean his toddler's sticky face with a damp washcloth. Tracey Ashford's golden-brown hair, long and thick and curly, was pulled back from her face and fastened behind her neck with a tortoiseshell clasp. Wispy bangs and a few stray strands framed soft brown eyes and a pert nose lightly sprinkled with freckles.

Tracey shot him a skeptical look and continued her task without commenting, as if she hadn't even heard him. Grant's eyes slid slowly over the rest of her.

Showered and dressed, Grant had planned an early start for his office in Columbia, South Carolina. From the looks of her, Tracey hadn't had time to do more than wash her face and slip on her white cotton robe.

She pushed her gold, wire-framed glasses up on the

bridge of her nose. Her challenging glance at him was accompanied by a hassled puff of breath, which blew the middle of her bangs dancing into the air.

Finally she said, "Oh, please, Grant. If I said yes, you'd have a panic attack right there in that spot." She shot him a frown, then scrubbed Kimberly's tiny fingers clean.

As Tracey leaned over the table, her robe fell open at the top, exposing a glimpse of the silky ecru gown beneath and an alluring touch of cleavage. Grant's gaze swept over the gentle swells of her firm breasts, hidden by a wisp of lace that would taunt any man's imagination.

The belt of her robe emphasized her small waist and gently rounded hips. It gaped open at her knee, exposing her shapely calf and ankle. She was barefoot, her toenails painted pink. She looked like a woman who'd just been pleasured by a man, soft all over and still a little sleepy-eyed.

Stunned by the direction of his thoughts, Grant diverted his attention to the mug of steaming coffee in his hand and away from the woman who more than occasionally baby-sat his children. As if it had free will, his gaze strayed back to her.

Studying her over the rim, he absently sipped from the mug. A slow-burning coil of fire ignited in his belly, and his chest grew heavy and congested. His entire body seemed to be coming alive after more than a year of celibacy.

"You think so?" Leaning his hip against the counter, he assumed an air of casualness. Grant wondered how many times he'd witnessed this scene without thinking of Tracey as a desirable woman.

Okay, he thought logically, he hadn't been with a woman in a long time.

A really long time.

So that had to be it. Since his divorce he hadn't *wanted* sex. He'd needed it a time or two, but he'd determinedly clamped down on his body's basic urges. He never wanted to be taken for a fool again. Just the memory of his disastrous marriage was enough to make him think twice about getting involved with another woman.

"I know so," Tracey answered, casting him a reproving glance.

"You don't know me as well as you think." Grant's tone was taunting as he tried his best to get a rise out of her. "I'd marry you in a minute if you said yes." That idea brought on lustful thoughts that made him wonder about his sanity.

Sure, when they'd been teens, he'd thought a time or two about what it would be like to make it with Tracey. What guy wouldn't have? She'd been pretty and outgoing, and Grant had often been conscious of guys who were after her.

Because of their deep friendship and his respect for her, he'd never infringed on the special bond they shared. Admittedly, he'd stepped slightly out-of-bounds a couple of times, but he'd never seriously put a move on her.

Suddenly he felt as if he was on a frozen pond and the ice was cracking beneath his weight. The tight awareness that started in his gut began to spread outward and down, heating the blood that rushed to his masculinity. Self-consciously, he shifted his body.

It had been a long time since Grant had felt lust,

and he wasn't particularly thrilled that his libido had shifted into high gear because of Tracey.

He and Lisa had fought during the better part of their five-year marriage and even more so the last year they were together. It had actually come as a surprise when she'd gotten pregnant, because they hadn't had sex very often toward the end of their marriage. When he'd suspected she was having an affair, Grant had stopped caring about sharing intimacies with her.

Though he'd never given Tracey's sexual habits much attention, thinking about them now didn't exactly sit well with him. She'd dated only a few times since her husband had died. No one seriously, though, and that told Grant just how much she missed Richard.

Thinking about her with Richard had never bothered him before, so Grant wondered why it did now. She was his best friend, so naturally he cared about her. She didn't have Richard anymore, and Grant had easily fallen back into the role of treating her like a little sister.

"Please," she begged. "It's too early in the morning for this." Her eyes locked on his with a promise of retaliation.

Grant shot her a disarming smile. "I'm as serious as a heart attack."

"Oh, give me a big break." She elaborated each word and gave him an I-know-you-too-well look. "You, sir, are just interested in all the free services I provide."

"Free services?" Grant choked out the words and nearly spilled coffee on his suit as forbidden images of hot kisses and naked, writhing bodies passed through his mind. Fine beads of sweat broke out across his forehead.

"Cooking, cleaning, baby-sitting, etcetera, etcetera," she recited haughtily. "I'm here more often than I'm at home. I have a workshop in one of the spare bedrooms. I might as well move in."

Yeah, you can move right into my bedroom.

Grant ordered himself to get a grip. This was Tracey, his longtime friend. She's like a sister to you, he reminded himself.

"Yeah," he agreed, attempting a sly grin, but not quite sure he managed one. "But you love it, and you know it."

Tracey's gaze bounced off him to his thirteen-month-old daughter. "You know how much I love you and the girls. I'd do anything for you." Her heavy-lidded gaze swung back to him, her expression serious.

"I know."

They stared at each other in stark silence, the tension between them building like lightning during a late-evening summer storm. Babbling noises from the high chair finally drew Tracey's attention, and she turned her gaze in the baby's direction.

Something within Grant's hardened heart stirred when he saw the way Tracey looked at his children. Her devotion overwhelmed him. She had never failed him. Not once.

Tracey had never gotten along well with Lisa. They'd gone to the same school but had never been friends. Lisa hadn't understood his friendship with Tracey.

Grant had done his best to hold on to his marriage, until he'd caught Lisa cheating on him. They'd already started divorce proceedings when his wife found out she was pregnant. Grant had insisted on a paternity test. When it was proven the child was his, he'd made an offer to pay her handsomely if she'd give him the baby. His wife had readily agreed.

Uncomfortable with the silence in the room, Grant said, "Maybe I really should marry you and make an honest woman of you." His cocky grin belied the emotions he was trying to deal with.

Tracey leaned over and picked the baby up from the high chair. An eyeful of smooth, milky skin swelled above the lacy edge of her nightgown, and Grant nearly groaned out loud.

"You'd better stop talking such nonsense," she reprimanded gently. "Kimmie's too young to understand what you say, but Stephanie certainly isn't. At four she comprehends a lot more than you think." She looked up and smiled sweetly when she saw the chagrined look on his face.

"You find being compromised amusing?" Grant walked over and took the baby from her.

"Hardly. Occasionally sleeping here doesn't compromise me, and you, of all people, know it," she said, poking her finger in his chest. She walked to the sink and rinsed out the washcloth, then laid it on the counter.

Grant had a hard time keeping housekeepers, and each time one quit, he called on Tracey. She was always happy to help him out. Often, whenever he had to work late, she would spend the night to make it easier on them both.

"Maybe not in our eyes," Grant said, trying to recover from the blow to his ego, "but my neighbor gives me a dirty look whenever you stay over."

"She does not!" Tracey looked at him to see if he was teasing, as she leaned her hip against the counter and took a sip of her coffee.

"It wasn't the first time, either," he confessed.

Tracey's chuckle made the idea sound absolutely ludicrous. "Why haven't you told me this before?" she asked.

Grant shrugged, and a disturbed frown creased his features. "I don't know. It didn't seem important."

Her soft laughter still echoed through the room. He didn't see what she thought was so damn funny! His nose slightly out of joint, he deliberately baited her. "If you feel your reputation's been sullied, my proposal stands."

"Yeah, right." Tracey breathed a deep sigh, and her heart gave a little lurch.

She *knew* Grant was goading her. There was no way on earth he could know how she really felt about him. He couldn't. She had never given him any idea.

Years ago when he'd met and married Lisa, Tracey had put her love for Grant in a safe place in her heart. At that time she'd told herself that her feelings for Grant were the result of a crush, that she'd get over him.

Only she never did.

She'd compared every man she'd met to Grant, even the man she'd married. She wasn't proud of that. Tracey had tried to give Richard her best, but there had been something missing in their marriage. She now knew she'd never loved him the way she should have. Guiltily she wondered if he'd ever known.

Her gaze slowly made its way over Grant's hard-muscled length. His hair was jet-black, his deep-set eyes a striking blue that would pale a clear summer sky. Tall and sexy, he lounged against the counter with the look of the devil himself in his indolent gaze. His dark-blue suit accentuated his olive complexion. No man had any business looking that handsome the first thing in the morning.

"Come on, give a guy a break," he pleaded, juggling the baby who was squirming to be put down.

"No, I'm afraid I must refuse, but thank you so very much for asking," she said, sounding very much like Cinderella turning down the handsome prince. Fresh emotions assailed her, and she allowed herself a private moment, wishing in her heart that he meant it, that he loved her the way she needed to be loved by him. Then she quickly banished such hopeless thoughts from her mind.

Grant had told her, the day his divorce became final, that he would never trust his heart to love again. Tracey had never forgotten how adamant he'd been that day, and there was no doubt in her mind that he meant it. He'd repeated his vow often over the past year.

She saw his jaw tighten a fraction. "I didn't mean to bruise your masculinity."

Grant's face became solemn. "My feelings are the least of my worries," he confessed.

Tracey knew that Grant felt he hadn't been the best of fathers. He worried constantly because his children didn't have a mother and that traveling for his job kept him away from home too much. He'd hired a number of housekeepers to take on the job of caring for them, but they'd quit.

Often he'd told Tracey what it had been like to grow up without his parents around. His father had been cold and distant and traveled a lot with his job. He'd been away more often than at home.

Because Grant's mother had died when he was six, he was raised by an array of sitters until he'd turned ten, which was when he started taking care of himself. He'd always told Tracey how lucky she was to have a mother and a father who loved her.

Watching the play of emotions on Grant's face, Tracey bit her lip and wished she'd been more careful. He was a good father and provided for his children as best he could.

She looked at Grant, and sadness filled her. "I'm sorry. I didn't mean—"

"I know, Trace." His expression was grim, his eyes filled with the kind of pain and resentment that destroyed the soul. "It's just so damned hard."

Raising two children alone, knowing that one day they'd find out their mother hadn't wanted them, made each day a living hell for him.

"You need to get over what Lisa did to you, Grant. She didn't deserve you. Are you going to let her destroy your whole life?"

"Tracey." Grant's tone warned her to back off. "This isn't about Lisa."

"It isn't?" Tracey questioned, pinning him with a stare that questioned his denial.

"I'm worried about the girls," he confessed. "I wish I could be with them more. They need some stability."

"You're doing the best you can for them, Grant," Tracey reassured him, her eyes soft and tender with concern. She took the baby from him.

"I couldn't do it without you."

"Well, you don't have to worry about me. I'm here for all of you as long as you need me."

Glancing at the clock on the microwave, she said, "Why don't you see if Stephanie's awake? You're going to be late if you don't get moving."

Grant left the room, and while he was checking on Stephanie, Tracey took Kimberly into the den and settled her in the playpen. With dark hair and deep-set blue eyes, both of his daughters looked an awful lot like their father. There was hardly a trace of their mother in them. That was a good thing, Tracey thought. Grant didn't need two daily reminders of his ex-wife. Neither did she, considering that she was with them so much.

Thinking she had time to dress, Tracey hurried toward the bedroom she used when she stayed over. She was startled when she rounded a corner and slammed right into Grant. He caught her in his arms to steady her, and she looked up at him, slightly breathless. Their gazes collided, and for a split second neither of them uttered a word. Her hands pressed against his shoulders.

"Whoa! Where are you going in such a hurry?" Grant knew he was playing with fire when he tightened his embrace and locked his arms around Tracey. It had been a long time since he'd held a woman this close, and she felt soft all over and warm to his touch. Her pliant body molded his from his chest to his thighs.

"Grant!" Tracey groaned and wiggled against him. Her breasts, crushed against his chest, bulged upward, swelling her cleavage provocatively. "Come on, let me go!"

She looked up and met his gaze. Her hair had fallen

in her face and Grant found himself brushing it back so he could look into her eyes. Her lashes lowered before he could read her thoughts.

"What's the matter? It isn't as if we're strangers." Her thin robe and nightgown made her feel nearly naked against him, and Grant stifled a groan. He was definitely losing it. He looked from her face to her full breasts and wondered what it would be like to gently massage them with his hands, to take them in his mouth.

"Grant!" Tracey exclaimed again, looking appalled as she caught the direction of his gaze. The balls of her hands shoved against him. "Let me go," she pleaded.

Grant was in deep trouble. His thoughts were getting way out of control. It was as if he'd awakened this morning and discovered Tracey was a living, breathing, absolutely enticing woman. She felt too good in his arms, supple and female, with curves just right for a man's touch.

His touch.

Tracey's eyes flashed to his. Grant often teased her, and this was just another way for him to get to her if she let him, which she couldn't afford to do. She'd realized a long time ago that she would never have Grant's love. She couldn't let herself wish, not even for a moment, that it was possible for him to care for her beyond friendship.

"Daddy, why are you hugging Tracey?" Huge, innocent blue eyes stared up at them.

Both adults were startled when Stephanie spoke. Grant immediately set Tracey away from him.

"Sweetheart, I was just teasing Tracey," he replied.

Tracey cast Grant a wary glance. He was smiling devilishly at her now, and suddenly she felt quite foolish. He'd admitted that he was just having fun with her. A hot flush rose in her cheeks, and she was glad she hadn't overreacted and said something totally stupid. She would have made a real fool of herself.

Grant followed Tracey into the kitchen where she gave Stephanie breakfast. Then she looked briefly at Grant and asked, "Are you going to be late tonight?"

"I hadn't planned on it. Why?"

"I have a date. I need to leave here by five to get back to my place and dressed," she told him. Her gaze flitted to him for a moment to check his reaction.

"With Edwards?"

"What?" Tracey stopped running the water and turned to look at him. He was sitting at the table, slouched back comfortably in his chair. He'd poured another cup of coffee and was raising it to his lips, eyeing her over the brim.

"Are you seeing Edwards?" he asked again, a slight edge to his voice. He took a drink from the cup, but his eyes never left hers.

"Yes," she answered and held her breath. Tracey had only been out with Morgan Edwards on two dates, but Grant hadn't liked Morgan since she'd introduced them, and he made no bones about telling her. With her head turned away, she silently mouthed his standard reply as he spoke.

"I don't know what you see in that guy." Grant down put his cup so hard on the table that his hot coffee spilled.

"I don't know why you don't like him. He's very nice," Tracey quietly replied, stilling her movements and glancing at him over her shoulder.

Grant grunted. "For one thing he's too damn old for you."

"We're just friends," she insisted. "What difference does it make, anyway? And may I remind you that a lot of women date older men. It isn't unheard of, you know."

"Well, you could find someone better suited to you." Grant stood up and approached her.

"You seem to find something wrong with every man I go out with." Tracey went back to viciously scrubbing a stain in the sink. As usual Grant was being overprotective. He seemed to feel it was his duty to watch over her and approve of every man she dated. He'd done it ever since she'd known him, but with closer scrutiny after her husband's death.

"You haven't been out with that many," he reasoned.

"I'm a grown woman, Grant," Tracey reminded him sternly.

Grant grimaced. *That* was the crux of his problem.

Two

Grant watched Tracey leave the room to check on Kimberly. Though part of his dislike of Edwards stemmed from Grant's sudden interest in Tracey as a woman, he didn't want to see her get hurt. He remembered only too well the night she'd called to tell him that Richard had been killed in an automobile accident on the way home from work. Her husband's death had been hard on her.

Grant would never forget the sound of her heart-wrenching sobs when he'd comforted her. He'd held her until she'd cried herself to sleep; then he'd put her to bed and sat up watching her most of the night. That had been just after his divorce, and Grant was glad he'd been able to be there for Tracey.

His heart had turned to stone; hers had been suddenly shattered. They'd leaned on each other to get through their pain.

He had to admit that Tracey was right about the way he felt about Edwards. Grant didn't really like the man. He was a lot older than Tracey. She needed someone closer to her own age, he thought.

Someone like him.

Grant stopped that thought process before it went any further. He had to get control over these new feelings for Tracey. Still, he wanted to know how much Tracey liked Edwards.

When she came back into the room, Grant broached the subject carefully. "I'm sorry I upset you."

Tracey faced him, the speculation in her expression telling him she doubted his words. With a shrug of her shoulders she said, "I'm not upset. You just need to realize that I don't need a guardian."

Grant sent Stephanie off to dress, then looked at Tracey and said, "I know your personal life is none of my business." Accusing eyes stared back at him, making him feel even more regretful.

He remembered Tracey's marriage to Richard. They'd seemed happy the three years they'd been to-gether. Tracey had once told Grant that she wanted to start a family by the time she was twenty-three, but she and Richard hadn't had any children. Tracey had mentioned that they'd been trying for a while before Richard's death.

Curiosity overriding his regret, he asked, "Do you ever think of getting married again?"

"Sometimes," Tracey replied, not really looking at him.

"To Edwards?"

That brought her gaze swiftly to his. "Grant, don't be ridiculous. We've only been out a couple of times," she said impatiently. "Why all the questions?" She took her cup to the sink and washed it out.

He tilted his head, thinking about it. "I don't know," he answered. "Just curious, I guess." Hearing her admit that she'd even thought about getting married again was like suddenly facing his worst fears.

"I guess I miss being married sometimes," she said wistfully. Tracey knew she hadn't truly loved Richard the way she should have, and she felt bad about that.

She took a deep breath, wishing she hadn't let the conversation get this far. Over the years she'd struggled with her feelings and she finally resolved to herself that she would never love another man the way she loved Grant. But she had to get on with her life, because she would never have Grant's love.

"I'm not on a manhunt, though. Maybe I'll get married again someday. I don't know."

"At least you didn't make a mistake the first time around," Grant said cynically.

"Like you when you married Lisa?" Tracey asked.

Grant didn't answer. He just stood there, his eyes fixed on some object across the room.

Tracey knew Grant had wanted Lisa from the moment he'd met her. She'd had the features of a model and the looks of a siren. Too late Grant had discovered that she had the heart of a snake. Tracey remembered when they'd started dating. It was at the beginning of her senior year. She and Lisa were both eighteen and Grant had been in his last year of college. When he'd found out Lisa was pregnant, he'd insisted on doing the right thing and marrying her.

It hadn't been easy for Grant, those first few years. He'd had to juggle marriage, a baby and a new job, but he'd worked hard at it. Apparently a lot harder than his wife.

Tracey looked at Grant. "Sometimes I feel as though life is passing me by," she admitted. "If Richard and I had had a baby—" She let her words drop off, unable to continue.

"I know how much you wanted a baby," Grant murmured.

"I don't want to talk about this anymore." Tracey's tone warned him to drop the subject.

Grant walked over and gently grasped Tracey's shoulders. She stiffened, the muscles in her arms tightening beneath his palms. He ran a hand around the back of her neck and massaged it.

Tracey knew he sympathized with her. He understood because he knew how it felt to live with soul-deep hurt. They both did.

She tilted her neck, giving in to the sensation of his warm hands against her skin.

Finally he offered gently, "Tracey, I know you miss Richard. It takes time to get over something like that."

She wasn't thinking of Richard at the moment. "Sometimes I feel that I'm running out of time," she confessed.

Grant's hands tightened on her shoulders. "You're only twenty-four."

Her heart aching, Tracey shrugged Grant's hands off, then tried to control the depression pulling at her. Grant could say that. He had two children to cherish and love.

"Come on, Trace. Don't be like that," Grant

coaxed. He stepped closer to Tracey and braced his hands against the counter on both sides of her, effectively pinning her in without actually touching her. Concern filled his blue eyes.

Tracey didn't move a muscle. She hadn't thought it possible to be so near someone without actually touching them. Grant's face was close to hers, and the familiar scent of his woodsy aftershave drifted to her. She tried not to breathe, tried not to acknowledge how strong and lean and threateningly masculine he was.

She'd always been a little in awe of this man, her best friend, of his devastating charm and personality, of his blatant sexuality and the power he wielded over women of all ages.

And she'd loved him with all her heart, she acknowledged silently to herself. She'd thought she'd put that love to rest. Grant had never been meant for her. He thought of her as his friend. It was past time for her to accept that.

"Are you okay?" he asked quietly, his deep tone disturbing the shadowed silence of the room.

"Yes, I'm fine," she answered stiffly. "Can we please change the subject?"

"You're a beautiful woman, Trace," Grant said suddenly. "Warm and loving. You have a lot to offer the right man."

Except you're the right man for me and you don't know it, her mind taunted.

"Grant." There was a lethal warning in her tone that was meant to caution him. She was becoming increasingly irritated by the topic of conversation. "I don't badger you about your personal life."

"I'm not seeing anyone for you to badger me

about," Grant qualified, his voice disturbingly calm, his eyes avoiding hers.

"My point exactly!" Tracey stated. The few times Grant had been out socially over the past year could be counted on one hand. When business had required his attendance at evening functions, she'd been the one to accompany him.

She knew the day would come when he would start dating. At twenty-eight he still had a long life before him—whether he believed it or not.

"I'm perfectly happy with things the way they are," Grant answered. He shoved his hands in his pockets and glowered at her, looking irritated because she'd turned the discussion around on him.

Tracey touched his cheek. His clean-shaven jaw tightened beneath her palm. His skin was smooth and soft to her touch, and her hand trembled ever so slightly.

"I know, but I can't live in limbo forever. And neither can you. You have to start thinking about making a new life for yourself and the girls." The words caused her heart to ache, but she wanted what was best for Grant and his daughters. His little girls needed a mother.

Grant had carried his pain like a shield, using it to keep women at arm's length. Today his armor had slipped a bit. He knew he had no right interfering in Tracey's personal life, but he couldn't stop himself.

That tight feeling inside his gut had grown until it threatened to cut off his air supply. He swallowed hard, indecision battling against a sensual pull that was close to consuming him.

What kind of reaction would he get from Tracey if he gave in to the desire to possess her mouth? Her lips looked hot and sweet. With an inward groan, he decided he needed some breathing space before he lost total control of the situation.

"Just drop it, Trace," he told her, his voice brooking no argument. Abruptly he moved away and snatched his keys from the counter, not trusting himself a moment longer. "I've gotta go. I'll do my best to get home by five."

"Thanks," Tracey answered, feeling as though he'd closed up on her and not understanding why. They'd always been able to talk about anything. Anything but his feelings about Lisa.

Standing at the kitchen window, Tracey watched Grant drive away, wondering why he'd suddenly felt it necessary to put this emotional distance between them. Turning, she went into the spare room, hoping to finish the stained-glass picture she'd started several weeks ago. With the delivery date fast approaching, she had a lot of work ahead of her.

Tracey's mother had worked with stained glass as a hobby for years, and Tracey had been allowed to watch and help when she was old enough to learn. After high school, Tracey started a business of her own, designing and finishing small paintings, windows, tiffany lamp shades and other assorted items.

Some of her things were in local shops, and she sold many custom pieces by word of mouth. The uniqueness of her work brought her a good income, and an inheritance from her grandparents afforded her the opportunity to have her own business. She loved the freedom of working at her own pace, and she was grateful she had plenty of time to devote to Grant and his girls.

Remembering Grant's impromptu proposal of the

morning, Tracey sighed as she worked on an intricate piece of indigo glass.

He was always teasing her. Usually she enjoyed their bantering.

Not today.

When Grant arrived at work, he was told that the president of his company wanted to see him. There was nothing peculiar in Robert Babcock's request. More often than not, his summons indicated problems had occurred in one of their locations in another part of the country.

Grant's specialty was troubleshooting and taking over until new management decisions could be made. He quickly covered the short distance to Robert's office.

An unexplainable tension pulled at him as he stepped into his employer's office. His eyes went directly to his boss as he closed the door quietly behind him. Robert sat behind an immense desk, his head bent over a mass of paperwork.

"Grant, come in and sit down," he said, looking up as Grant walked in.

Grant settled in one of the high-backed leather chairs directly in front of the solid oak desk. Sitting back, he crossed an ankle over his knee.

He examined the lines of anxiety in Robert's face with a careful, almost guarded expression. Grant's shoulders tensed, and an uneasy feeling crawled up his spine.

"Problems?" Grant prompted, curious to know what had his boss on edge. He'd been Robert's right-hand man for the past four years.

Robert leaned back in his chair. "I received a call

from Jim McLaney in Atlanta this morning. He's taking an early retirement due to health reasons. His doctor has advised him to quit immediately.''

Grant nodded, appreciating Robert's predicament.

''I know this isn't the best time for you, but the circumstances are beyond my control. You know we're under contract negotiations, and it's crucial that we present a solid position so as not to set back arbitration. We've got a ten-million-dollar contract due.''

''I can be ready to leave by tomorrow,'' Grant said, knowing Tracey would take care of the girls.

Robert sat forward and looked Grant straight in the eyes. ''Good. I want you to take over the Atlanta division.''

''No problem. How long will it take before you fill Jim's position?'' Grant asked. Babcock Enterprises was a major distributor of electronic parts on the East Coast. The Atlanta office and factory were the second largest of their five divisions.

Robert looked speechless for a moment, then his lips formed an amused smile. ''I don't think you understand. I'm offering you the vice presidency.''

Grant's expression became serious as the enormity of the offer became crystal clear.

''I've made no secret of my confidence in your ability to perform for this company,'' Robert admitted. ''I knew from the moment you were hired it was only a matter of time before I moved you into a top position.

''The problem is I need someone there permanently, within the month. As it is, I've instructed Jim to delegate most of his work load to Dean Garrison, his second in command, and to handle only high-priority matters until he's replaced.''

Grant knew Garrison, having worked with him before. Though rumors abounded about the man's prowess with women, he was a top-notch executive.

"I don't know, Robert. The girls—I'd have to see if I could work something out. You know I've had a tough time keeping someone to take care of them on a regular basis. Tracey has them today because I just lost another housekeeper. The move wouldn't even be a problem if I knew she'd be there to help me.''

Until that moment, Grant hadn't realized that taking the job would also mean separating himself, as well as his children, from Tracey. He stretched his neck, trying to ease some of the tension building there.

"Maybe you can talk her into going with you,'' Robert suggested. "It's not as if she couldn't do her work in another city. After the anniversary piece she did for me, I couldn't give her name and number out fast enough.''

"I couldn't ask her to do that,'' Grant answered.

Or could he?

Grant banished the thought as soon as it popped into his mind. He couldn't take advantage of Tracey that way.

"Well, in any case, Grant, I'm willing to work with you in whatever way I can. Dean's a good man and can handle matters temporarily. Give it some thought. I'd like to know as soon as you come to a decision—the sooner the better.''

Grant turned toward him. "You'll be the first to know. I appreciate your confidence in me.''

Grant returned to his office, his mind already swimming with the difficult decision that lay before him.

Hours later Grant glanced at his watch, then sat back in his chair. He hadn't realized how late it had become. The drive home would take at least forty minutes, depending on rush hour traffic. Tracey had said she wanted to leave by five, and Grant knew he would never make it home on time.

With a disgusted sigh he reached for the telephone and punched a number to speed dial his home, unsure of the welcome his call would receive. When Tracey picked it up, she sounded winded.

"Tracey, it's Grant."

"Shouldn't you be on your way home by now?"

"That's why I'm calling. I was just about to leave, which means I'm not going to get there on time. I just thought I'd warn you."

"Don't worry about it. I called and canceled with Morgan for tonight," she told him. She sounded uneasy.

"You did?" It shouldn't have pleased him so much.

"Stephanie isn't feeling well, and I don't want to leave her."

"What's wrong with Stef?" Grant asked.

"I'm not sure," Tracey admitted, frustration in her tone. "She has a slight cough and says her chest hurts. Maybe she's coming down with a cold." Her voice was hesitant, as if she doubted that possibility.

Grant let out a deep breath, hoping it wasn't something more. First the offer of a promotion, now this. Why did everything have to happen at once?

"Tracey, you didn't have to cancel," he told her,

a rough edge to his voice as he began to worry about his daughter.

"I know, but I thought you might need my help. You don't mind, do you?"

"Of course not. Look, I'm just about to leave. Why don't I pick up something for dinner? I can stop at that Chinese place down the street on the way home."

"I've already started dinner, buster, so just get home before it's done."

"I'll do my best."

Tracey hung up the phone, anxious to see Grant. Stephanie had been feeling bad all afternoon, and Tracey was worried. She wondered what could be wrong with the child, then told herself not to get worked up. Kids got sick all the time. It was nothing to be nervous about. But Stephanie was usually a very healthy little girl. Kimmie was prone to ear infections, but Stephanie had a resistance to bugs that, until today, was astonishing.

Thirty minutes later Tracey heard the automatic garage door open, then the engine of Grant's car as he drove in. It had been a long afternoon, and she was glad he was home. His children needed him.

Tracey needed him, too. She needed his assurance that Stephanie's illness wasn't something serious.

She might as well have wished for the moon. Tracey didn't have to look at Grant to know he wasn't in a pleasant mood. As he walked into the den, he shrugged off his suit jacket and tossed it across a chair. The creases in his forehead were pronounced, and deep brackets framed the scowl on his lips.

Tracey was in no mood to deal with whatever was bothering Grant. She was tired and worried, and the fact that the dinner she'd prepared was overcooked wasn't helping her frame of mind. When her eyes met his, she tried hard to keep her tone from sounding abrupt.

"Bad day?"

"Yeah." He sighed, sounding as frazzled as he looked. He tugged at the tie around his neck, then unbuttoned the collar of his white dress shirt with one hand. As if he was trying to convince her, the fingers of his other hand massaged his right temple.

"How's Stef?" he asked.

"She doesn't have a fever, but she said her head hurts. She's sleeping right now. I've already fed Kimmie, and she's in her playpen."

Grant's eyes narrowed on Tracey as she sat on the overstuffed brown leather sofa. He could tell that her day had been as tough as his. He was glad he had her to depend on, but hated feeling obligated to her. It was another reminder to him of how much his kids needed a mother.

Just looking at Tracey made his head spin, and that crazy, out-of-place feeling swiftly attacked his body, starting in his chest, then moving toward his stomach. Swallowing hard, Grant closed his eyes to block out the sight of her.

"Why don't you go on home, Trace?" he suggested. Grant knew he didn't sound very grateful, but right now he really needed to banish thoughts of his attraction to Tracey from his mind. Alone with her in his house, he couldn't seem to think straight.

Tracey shook her head, and an array of golden-brown curls bounced about her shoulders. "I thought I'd spend the night, just in case you need me."

"You don't have to stay." That he needed her wasn't debatable. Frustrated, he just wasn't sure that he'd be able to keep his hands off her if she stayed all night again at his house.

"I know," Tracey answered on a harsh whisper. She uncurled her legs and stood. "I told Stephanie I'd be here in the morning."

Grant shrugged. "Suit yourself."

Casting him a hard look, Tracey turned and went into the kitchen.

Grant followed close behind her.

"Dinner's been ready," she announced in a tone that told him she didn't appreciate his being late. She raised her arms and stretched, then started moving about the kitchen.

When she arched her back, her breasts jutted out and up, drawing Grant's gaze. Her blue jeans were well worn and fit her tush and legs like a second skin. She had on one of his old dress shirts, provocatively unbuttoned part of the way down, the tails tied about her waist.

"Do you need any help?" He hoped not. Grant knew he was in deep trouble. He'd been sexually aware of Tracey from the moment he'd walked in the door. What he needed most was to get out of the kitchen and take a cold shower.

When she looked up at him, he dropped his gaze to the floor. He felt like a fool.

"No, I'll just put it on the table."

"I'll go wash up." Grant left the room without looking at her. A cold shower—yes, that's exactly what he needed. It was a real shame he didn't have time for one.

Three

Grant stood at the bathroom sink and thought about how, in one day, his whole life had turned upside down. On his way home he'd done nothing but think about Robert's offer.

He knew he would be out of his mind to uproot his life and move to Atlanta. The girls had barely started adjusting to living without their mother, and it wasn't fair to throw them another curve. As well, Stephanie would be starting kindergarten soon. Why on earth did the promotion have to come now?

Though it disgusted him, part of him felt resentful at the thought of turning down the opportunity for advancement. He'd worked damned hard toward this goal. Knowing it was finally within his reach and that he might have to decline the promotion really stung.

His long hours at work always meant a lot of time away from his daughters. Could he take them away from the only people they knew and who loved them and settle them in a new house with yet another stranger to care for them while he was working? What other alternative could there be?

Tracey.

His mind seemed set on coming back to Tracey as an answer to his problems. Sure, she loved Stephanie and Kimberly, but would it be fair to ask her to leave her home and family and follow him to Atlanta?

What could he offer her as an inducement?

A home? A place in his life, in the lives of his children? She had that now. Would that be enough for her to decide to go with them? Grant didn't think so. Tracey needed more, some personal incentive, something permanent, to induce her into going with him.

Marriage and a family of her own.

She'd said as much this morning. Would she consider marrying Grant and being a mother to his children, whom she already loved?

Marry him?

The idea sounded foreign even as it crossed his mind. Did he want to get married again? Until this morning he'd believed he never wanted another woman in his life.

At least not permanently.

But marriage to Tracey would be safe. His feelings for Tracey were based on friendship, not romance. He wouldn't have to give her his heart. And better yet, she wouldn't expect him to. They would be friends and, of course, eventually lovers. Tracey knew how he felt about love; she wouldn't expect it of him. And he knew Tracey would never let herself care for another man the way she had Richard.

Grant washed his face and patted it dry. He felt as if he was carrying an enormous burden, and Stephanie's unexpected illness seemed like another responsibility on his shoulders.

As Grant returned to the kitchen, Tracey was removing baked chicken from the oven. She placed it on the table.

A harsh silence fell over the room like a dark, thunderous cloud. They each took their seats and filled their plates. The clanking of dinnerware seemed ridiculously loud in the rigid atmosphere.

Tracey glanced briefly at Grant as she passed him the dinner rolls. ''What's bothering you?'' she asked, curiosity arching her brow.

''Nothing.'' He stabbed a piece of chicken and forked it into his mouth, chewing mechanically, not really tasting it. Tracey frowned and looked away. Seeing her hurt expression, Grant reached for her hand. His thumb gently grazed the back of it.

''I'm sorry, Trace. It's been a hard day. I don't mean to be bad company.'' And he didn't know what in the hell was wrong with him.

Touching her was a tactical mistake he hadn't meant to make. His body was already on fire. It seemed as if most of his blood converged in one particularly masculine area. He abruptly removed his hand and finished the last of his dinner, then sighed and pushed his plate away.

''Look, something came up at work, and I've been thinking about it all day. I have some things to work out. That's all,'' he explained.

''All right,'' Tracey said. ''But I'm here if you need me.''

Seeming on better terms, they cleaned the kitchen

together. While Tracey was finishing up, Grant left to do some work that he'd brought home. A couple of hours later he found Tracey in the kitchen making coffee. When he walked in, she turned to look in his direction.

Tracey studied Grant's expression with apprehension, knowing he had something on his mind, which accounted for his sullen mood at the dinner table.

"Join me in a cup of coffee?" She poured two cups even as she asked the question, then handed one to Grant. They sat facing each other at the table. Tracey stirred a teaspoon of sugar into the dark brew.

Grant's gaze lifted from his coffee, and Tracey's eyes met his. "Robert wants me to go to Atlanta before the end of the week. On Wednesday, probably."

"I see." Tracey took a sip of coffee from the cup, her expression thoughtful. "Why the forlorn expression? Is it because of Stephanie?"

"I'm worried about her, yes," Grant admitted, frowning. "This past year has been tough on the girls."

Tracey's hand touched his, her eyes softening. "They're doing okay."

Grant nodded his head. "I wish they didn't have to live like this. When my mom died, it was really hard for me. I missed her a lot." A disturbing sadness came over him. "My father never spoke of her. It was as if she was supposed to be wiped from my memory. I hate seeing my own children going through the same thing I did."

"The girls are adjusting," she said.

"Thanks to you and your parents."

"We love them."

Grant nodded and smiled just a little. "You won't mind taking care of them for me, then?"

"Of course not," Tracey assured him.

Grant's eyebrow rose. "What about Edwards?"

"What about him?" Her confusion was genuine.

"Are you seeing him again?"

Tracey shook her head. "Maybe, maybe not. I told you we're just friends."

Grant took his cup to the sink and dumped out the remainder of its contents. "I have about another hour of paperwork. Can I help you with anything before I get back to it?"

"No, you go ahead."

He nodded and left the kitchen. Tracey washed out the two cups and let them drain by the sink. Then she decided to change clothes and get ready for bed before watching a little television. She went to her room and peeled off her jeans. She removed her glasses, rolled up her sleeves, then washed her face and patted it dry.

Picking up her glasses reminded her that she had an appointment with the eye doctor in the morning. She slid them on, then changed into her nightgown and robe. After putting on her slippers, she went back to the den.

She flipped on the television and set the channel to a situation comedy, then sat back comfortably. Moments later she yawned. Resting her head on the arm of the sofa, she stretched out.

That's the way Grant found her—nestled on the sofa, her legs curled beneath her. He'd gone into the kitchen to get another cup of coffee and stopped dead in his tracks when he walked back through the den.

He glanced at his watch and was surprised it was after eleven. He'd forced himself to stay cooped up in his office away from Tracey until he could get a handle on what was going on inside him.

Grant walked over to Tracey and hesitated. The endearing picture she made tugged on his heart. Her hair fell around her face in disarray, and her glasses were askew. The fuzzy pink slippers on her feet brought a smile to his lips. It was then that he noticed her robe, loosely tied and gaping open, leaving very little to his imagination.

Grant's gaze fell to her breasts, and he saw the outline of her dark nipples beneath the fine silk. His body tightened. He had to will himself not to take advantage of the moment and let his hands seek the places they longed to touch.

Before temptation overtook him, he removed her glasses and laid them on the coffee table, then leaned over and scooped Tracey up in his arms. She moaned softly and buried her face in his chest.

As he carried her from the room, Grant tried to think of anything other than how it felt to hold her in his arms. In the room Tracey used at his house, he knelt at the edge of her bed, holding her in his lap as he turned back the covers.

She sighed softly, snuggling closer, and he bit his lip as he became rigid. Damn, how he wanted her! He wanted to bring her awake slowly with caressing hands and hot, wet kisses. He wanted to feel her silky skin, wanted to explore and taste every inch of her.

Before he lost what was left of his good sense, he eased her down, removed her slippers and tucked the soft covers over her without removing her robe. He didn't trust himself enough to do that.

Still, he couldn't bring himself to leave her. His hand brushed her hair from her face. His fingers lingered to touch her cheek where her lashes rested in soft semicircles. She stirred and turned her face toward his palm, her lips soft as they made contact with his skin.

The unsettled feeling that had been tugging at him all day attacked him again, now more like a raging inferno, sending shafts of desire coursing through him. His blood felt hot and thick in his veins, and his body felt as though it was on fire.

Grant went down on his knees beside the bed and put his face close to Tracey's. She smelled sweet, like wildflowers in a spring meadow. He figured she'd had a pretty rough day with the girls. She must have been worn-out to fall asleep on the couch.

He rubbed his thumb gently over her lips. She was sleeping so soundly she didn't even stir. Her lips were warm and Grant wanted to touch his mouth to hers.

He didn't allow himself to do so. He had a feeling that one brief, enticing taste of her would never be enough.

Hours later Tracey awoke with a start. Her body tensed when she realized she wasn't dreaming, that the harsh, rasping sounds she heard were very real. She jumped from the bed and raced toward the muffled noise as she tried to clear her sleep-fogged mind.

She headed straight for Stephanie's room where she thought the sounds were coming from, a terrible feeling of foreboding coming over her. Grant was right on her heels by the time she got there, and they instantly saw that the little girl was in distress.

Stephanie was barely breathing, her lungs struggling to suck in precious air, only to be denied, then forced to repeat the horrible ritual. She wasn't able to talk, and her eyes were wide with terror. Her small chest heaved, and the whistling sound in it grew louder and louder, more menacing as precious seconds ticked by. "I've got to get her to the emergency room!" Grant barked. "Wrap a blanket around her while I get my keys!" He didn't wait for a response, but bolted for the door and disappeared.

Tracey yanked the blanket from where it was tucked beneath the mattress. She scooped Stephanie up and hurried from the room. In the hallway, she nearly ran into Grant who'd already slipped on a shirt to go with the jeans he'd pulled on earlier. He didn't bother buttoning it as he put his sneakers on, his keys dangling from his teeth.

He gathered Stephanie close, and Tracey ran ahead of him toward the door to the garage, wanting desperately to go with him but knowing it was impossible because she had to stay with Kimberly.

Grant rushed out the back door.

"Call me!" Tracey screamed after him, huge tears burning her eyes.

"As soon as I can," Grant yelled back, settling Stephanie into the front seat of the station wagon. While Tracey pushed the button to open the garage door, Grant hustled to the driver's side, and the car roared to life. He backed out and took off, his tires squealing against the pavement.

Tracey stood and watched until the taillights faded from her sight, then closed the door. She quickly went to check on Kimberly and found her sleeping soundly, undisturbed by the trauma that had taken place moments ago. Satisfied the baby was all right, Tracey went to her room for her slippers, realizing she already had her robe on. She didn't remember going to bed. A warm flush crawled up her neck.

Grant must have carried her there.

It was three in the morning when Tracey heard the garage door open. She was at the door and down the few steps that led to the garage by the time Grant had gotten out and rounded the rear of the car, Stephanie tucked safely in his arms. Holding the small child against him with one arm, Grant opened the other one for Tracey as she ran to him, tears streaming down her cheeks.

"Is she all right?" she managed to ask.

"She's going to be fine," Grant said, and took a deep breath. "Let's get her to bed."

"Of course," Tracey whispered, wiping her eyes with the back of her hand. Through a haze of tears, she led the way to Stephanie's room. Grant put Stephanie to bed, and Tracey drew the covers over her, taking solace from the fact that the child seemed to be breathing normally.

"Come on, Trace," Grant called quietly. He tugged on her arm, and Tracey reluctantly allowed him to propel her from the room. "She should sleep now."

Tracey slowly followed Grant to the den. There, relief washed over her, and she collapsed against his rock hard chest, sighing heavily, wetting his shirt with even more tears. Grant gathered her in his arms, soothing her emotional release, caressing her back with his hands.

Meeting no resistance, Grant directed Tracey to the sofa where he sat, placing her next to him, then pulling her into his arms again. She went willingly, practically clinging to him.

When her tears and shaking finally subsided, she tried to pull away, but Grant resisted. It felt too good to hold someone, to have a warm body to share the nightmare with. She must have felt the same way because she hesitated, then sagged against him.

"What was wrong with her?" Tracey finally managed to ask, her voice sounding raspy from her bout of crying.

"Asthma," Grant answered, his own voice unsteady. He looked into Tracey's troubled eyes. "The doctor said it isn't unusual for a child to suddenly develop it. He also said it's possible she'll outgrow it."

"Will she be all right?" Tracey pressed closer to his chest and took a deep breath, her body convulsing with a slight shudder. Grant's arm tightened around her.

"He assured me she would. They gave her several shots to alleviate her distress. Eventually her breathing was under control and they ran a few tests. I had to answer a ton of questions, about me and what I knew about Lisa. I'm sorry I wasn't able to call you, but I didn't want to leave Stephanie alone."

"I...understand. I was just so worried," Tracey replied, her voice cracking.

"It's okay now, babe," he soothed, lifting her head and placing his cheek against hers.

"Oh, Grant," Tracey cried, her voice breaking, "I thought we were going to lose her." She trembled violently.

"I know." Grant brushed his lips against her brow, tugging her more securely against him. He knew what she was feeling, and his heart throbbed. "I was scared, too." For a frightening amount of the time that the doctor had examined Stephanie, he'd felt the same tormenting fear.

Tracey sniffed, and Grant smoothed a strand of her hair away from her face as he looked at her. She didn't have her glasses on, and her lashes were wet and matted together, glistening like sharp spikes of gold.

For a long moment neither of them seemed to breathe as their eyes met and their gazes held. Silently they regarded each other, unwilling to speak of emotions building inside them. Grant touched his lips to her forehead and murmured, "It's okay, Trace, she's safe now."

Grant's warm breath was so close to her mouth that Tracey's head involuntarily tilted up, bringing her lips dangerously close to his. A battle raged within her. She needed someone to hold her. Now, this very minute, to assuage her fears and comfort her, to make her feel that the nightmare was really over, that the little girl she loved so much was truly out of danger.

Grant slowly lowered his mouth, and his lips gently nudged Tracey's, tasting, savoring. He lifted his head and waited for a protest that never came. In the next moment his mouth settled on hers.

At the first touch of Grant's lips, Tracey went all liquid inside, her bones melting like wax under the hot desert sun. Her hand slipped behind his neck, her touch tentative, unsteady. His mouth was like a blazing fire, sending an inferno of wild desire spinning through her. Tracey strained toward him, aching to be closer to the molten heat of his body, her breasts brushing softly against his chest. Grant drew away from her and stared into her passion-filled eyes. Neither of them questioned the time or the place, nor the circumstances that brought her to him. Grant's gaze was one of supreme masculine awareness as he began to lower his mouth again.

"Open your mouth for me," he gently commanded, his lips against hers. Tracey complied and his tongue filled her mouth, finding hers waiting and wanting. He lured her tongue into his mouth and sucked it gently. She moaned low and deep in her throat, and the intimate, sexy sound seemed to make Grant's control snap. He loosened his hold on her long enough to get his hand between them and untie the sash of her robe. He spread it open and pulled her close again.

Her gown was whisper thin, and her pebble-hard nipples brushed his chest through the delicate fabric. He groaned and nudged her against the cushions of the sofa, levering his body over hers, kissing her fiercely.

Tracey was beyond any form of reasoning. Grant's lips, his hands, were making her feel things she'd never even dreamed possible. A warm, languid heat began to build deep inside her, zapping her ability to think and making her weak with need, with wanting. Her body arched against his, seeking fulfillment.

"Easy, babe, easy." He whispered the words in her ear, his voice low and seductive. Then his mouth was on hers again, hungrily, as if starved for the taste of her.

Tracey clung to him, her arms wrapped around him, holding him to her. He ran his tongue along her cheek to her ear, savoring the delicate pink shell. His teeth nibbled the flesh of her lobe, biting it gently.

His mouth was wet and hot, raining fiery kisses along
her neck, forging a path to the aching swells of her
breasts.

Tracey's hands weren't idle. They unbuttoned his
shirt, then slipped inside and stroked his skin. His
chest was hard muscled, his body warm as she slid
her palms over him, slipping his shirt off his shoulders. Grant struggled out of it as he kissed her again.

The agony Grant experienced at her touch was both
pleasurable and enticing. He groaned low in his throat
as her hands held his head in a viselike grip, guiding
his path, encouraging his sensual journey as he found
her breast.

His teeth grazed one nipple, his tongue wetting the
silky fabric of her gown. Tracey cried out softly and
arched her body toward the tantalizing warmth of his
mouth. Grant circled the hard bud with his tongue
while his hand found her breast and molded it.

Aching to taste what he'd been thinking about all
day, he slid the strap of her gown off her shoulder
and bared one full plump breast. When he lowered
his mouth and touched the hard peak with his tongue,
Tracey moaned and moved her hips against him in a
message of desire.

Grant murmured his pleasure and sucked harder,
pulling more of her into his mouth. Slowly he released all but the tiny bud, which he held captive
between his teeth.

"Grant," she hissed.

His name on her lips was like adding gasoline to a
raging bonfire. Grant's hands were all over her now,
caressing her rib cage, inching her gown up her
thighs, exposing her beige satin panties. He ran his
finger down her middle, then between her legs.

Her hips lifted against his hand as he touched her. Then he grasped her panties and slid them down her legs. He wanted to look at all of her, to see her go crazy for him, but Tracey was having none of it. She kissed him hungrily as her hands stroked shoulders and chest.

Grant moved his leg between hers, and her warmth seeped into him as her tongue played with his. Her hips rocked against his, causing him to harden even more. All he could think about was stripping off his clothes and sinking deep into her. He pushed against her hard, and she rewarded his efforts with a cry of desire.

A shrill scream suddenly entered their utopia, breaking through their fragile bond of intimacy. Tracey's eyes flew open in alarm, and suddenly she realized that she'd heard Stephanie crying out.

Tracey blinked, then stiffened as the awareness of where she was and what she and Grant were doing came to her. Her eyes widened in shock as they locked with Grant's. Mortified, she cringed and slammed her lids shut.

"Let me up!" she cried in a fit of panic.

"Trace—"

"Now!" She pushed at his chest with her elbows, then bucked against him with her body. She instantly regretted her impulsive movement. She could feel him hard and ready for her.

For her!

The thought exploded in her mind, bringing with it graphic pictures of how far out of control they had gone. Appalled, she burned with humiliation.

To her relief Grant rolled off her and quickly got to his feet. Frowning, he extended his hand to her, but Tracey scrambled off the couch under her own power, her legs shaking and barely able to carry her weight. She quickly made her way to Stephanie's room, gathering her robe about her and tying it as she went, realizing just how naked she was under it.

Stephanie was sitting up in bed, half-asleep and whimpering. Tracey rushed to her and gathered her close. Her legs nearly buckled, and she sat down on the bed and rocked the child back and forth. As soon as Stephanie began to calm down, she lowered her to the bed and stroked her back until she finally drifted off to sleep.

Grant was at the doorway, and Tracey could feel his eyes boring into her, but she couldn't bring herself to look at him. She went hot all over and was thankful the dim night-light prevented him from knowing.

She had no choice but to remember what had happened between them only moments ago. How could she have let Grant make love to her like that? Her heart thudded heavily against her chest. For years she'd hidden her true feelings from him, had never even hinted how much he meant to her.

And in a few moments of ecstasy, she might have jeopardized her relationship with him forever. How could she have been so stupid?

Tracey had been married, so she wasn't naive. She knew exactly where she and Grant were headed before they heard Stephanie's cries. Tracey hadn't even thought of stopping what they'd started. Had it not been for Stephanie interrupting them, Tracey knew that she and Grant would have made love.

What was she going to say to him? She had no excuse to offer for her behavior except that it had been an extremely emotional evening and they'd both needed someone warm and caring to turn to.

The fact that neither of them had dated seriously in the past year had to have something to do with their reactions to each other.

Of course, she told herself, that didn't mean Grant had been living without sex. He was a virile, handsome man. Though they'd never talked about it, she'd naturally assumed that he wasn't celibate.

With as much grace as she could muster, Tracey chose to ignore the incident between them, deciding to pretend as if the lustful scene on the couch had never taken place. Just thinking about the way she'd succumbed to the heat of his kisses made her tremble.

She took a deep breath and tried to regain enough composure to get past him. If she could only get to her bedroom, she'd be able to shut the door and escape any attempt he would make to discuss it.

She made it only as far as the door.

Grant was leaning his broad shoulder against the frame, blocking her path, forcing her to stop in front of him. From the intense look in his eyes, Tracey knew he had absolutely no intention of letting it drop.

"Please move. I'm going to bed," she whispered.

"Not just yet," he told her, his voice gentle, yet firm.

"Get out of my way."

"No."

"Grant—"

"It won't go away, Trace. We need to talk about it."

"I don't *want* to talk about it!" She stared at the floor, feeling as if she would burst into tears at any moment.

Grant reached toward her, and she jerked away from him just as quickly. Her head snapped up, and she aimed a piercing gaze at him.

"Get out of my way or I swear I'll walk out of this house right this minute and never come back!"

Four

Tracey knew there was no way on God's green earth she would leave while Stephanie wasn't feeling well, and she knew Grant realized it was an empty threat. Nevertheless, he stepped aside without saying a word.

Without glancing at him, Tracey moved past Grant and rushed to her room, quickly closing the door behind her. She didn't turn on the light as she climbed into bed and pulled the covers up to her neck.

Grant's room was next to hers, and she could hear him moving about. Burying her head beneath her pillow, she tried to block out the muffled sounds. Visions of his body, taut and perfect and half-naked, filled her mind.

Grant had always been her best friend. If Tracey thought there was any chance Grant could really and truly care for her as a woman, a partner for life, she'd be the happiest woman alive. But she knew better.

Grant was reacting to her as a woman. Any warm-blooded female would have gotten the same response from him, she told herself.

It was after four-thirty in the morning before sleep finally claimed her. Tracey awoke when she heard Kimberly playing in her crib.

Though she dreaded facing Grant, she knew it was inevitable. She quickly slipped on her clothes, anxious to see how Stephanie was feeling.

Evidently the trauma of the night before had taken its toll on the little girl, because she was still sleeping soundly when Tracey went in to check on her.

A short while later Tracey walked into the kitchen with the baby on her hip. She strapped Kimberly in her high chair, then started a pot of coffee, just as she'd done on many of the mornings she'd stayed over. Only this wasn't like any of the other mornings she'd spent in Grant's house.

This was the morning after she'd almost made love with him.

Since Grant's divorce, Tracey had felt completely at home in his house. Lisa's extravagant touch was evident throughout each room. Tracey sometimes wondered why Grant hadn't made some changes to banish his ex-wife's existence.

At this moment Tracey was only sure of one thing—she had betrayed the friendship and trust that she and Grant had shared for many years. She wanted to think that she would have eventually come to her senses and stopped making love with Grant before they crossed over a line that neither of them wanted to cross. But in her heart, she *knew* she wouldn't have.

Guilt besieged her, making her chest ache, bringing scorching-hot tears to her eyes. ''Oh, what have I done?'' she whispered aloud to herself, wondering how she'd be able to face Grant when he walked into the kitchen.

Tracey groaned and pressed fingertips to her temple. She was faced with realizing that she and Grant had stepped over an invisible border of their friendship. Could they go on and pretend that nothing had happened between them?

She stirred the scrambled eggs in the frying pan, going through the motions of preparing breakfast as if on automatic pilot. She knew too well that what happened between them would affect their relationship. She'd always wondered what it would be like to be in Grant's arms, to have him make love to her.

Now she knew.

Grant's kisses, his loving, had reached to the very core of her feelings for him, touching that secret place where her love had been hidden. She'd easily responded to each and every stroke of his gentle hands. For a moment she closed her eyes and let herself remember the pleasure she'd experienced. She could almost feel his hot tongue as it touched her breasts, his teeth as they grazed her nipples.

Stop! she told herself, opening her eyes and forcing herself to accept reality. Grant wasn't hers to have. He didn't want a relationship with a woman. Not a permanent, long-lasting, loving relationship. He'd made that clear many times. She had no delusions of Grant falling in love with her.

She scooped the eggs onto a plate, then separated a portion for Kimberly. As she fed the baby, she tried to decide how to handle the situation when Grant came down to breakfast.

* * *

Grant was a bit surprised to see Tracey's door already open when he got up. After the way she'd run from him last night, he'd expected her to barricade herself in her room to avoid facing him. After a quick shower, he dressed hurriedly, anxious to see Tracey and gauge her attitude toward him this morning.

Last night she wouldn't even look at him. He'd wanted to get it all out in the open, but she'd made it crystal clear she wanted no part of it. So he'd backed off, thinking that a little time couldn't possibly hurt anything.

Grant didn't even try to label his emotions. He wanted Tracey—the way a man wants a woman, hard and fast, slow and easy. He hadn't had sex since his divorce, hadn't really been interested...until yesterday, when he'd had to face his desire for Tracey.

Now his body was awakening from its self-imposed celibacy with a force that demanded to be reckoned with.

He felt as if he was becoming obsessed with having Tracey. He wanted to be deep inside her, to hear her moan with ecstasy, to feel her body writhe beneath his, to hear her beg him to take her.

So maybe offering Tracey marriage was the answer to several problems facing him. A rational, sensible relationship with her would be the perfect solution. He'd have a mother for his children and a woman in his bed.

He wouldn't have to love her or give her a part of himself. He'd learned that fate played rough. He wouldn't open his heart to love again.

Making love was quite another thing.

Making love to Tracey was what he wanted. He groaned savagely as he made his way toward the kitchen, his body tightening, his loins throbbing. He had to pause outside the door for a few minutes to muster some control over his salacious urges.

He entered the kitchen, and at first glance everything seemed completely normal. There was a pot of coffee brewing, and the distinct aroma filled the room. A cup was sitting in front of Tracey, steam still rising from it, indicating that she hadn't been there long. He noticed that her shoulders tensed slightly as he walked into the room.

The strained atmosphere served as a silent warning to him that things weren't quite as they seemed. Though Tracey didn't look up to acknowledge his presence, Grant felt her gaze on him when he turned his back and reached for a mug from the cabinet.

He circled the room and poured himself a cup of coffee. Then, with slow, deliberate movements, he planted himself in a chair directly across from her and gave her a long, speculative look.

She'd taken the time to dress in a red running suit that hid every luscious curve, and he couldn't help thinking she'd done so on purpose—as if he would be capable of forgetting the way his heart nearly stopped when he touched her silky skin, or the way he'd thought he'd died and gone to heaven when his mouth tasted her breast.

He assessed her outward appearance. She seemed to have taken great care in making herself look as plain and as undesirable as possible. Her hair had been thoroughly brushed and pulled back into a tight ponytail, causing her to look about seventeen. Evidently she'd found her glasses on the table in the den where he'd put them, because they sat primly just below the bridge of her nose.

Finally she flickered a wary glance in his direction. When she didn't make an attempt to speak, he broke the ice between them.

"How are you this morning?"

She jumped when she heard his voice, but seemed to recover quickly, still not looking directly at him.

"Fine." Tracey kept her eyes focused on the scrambled eggs in front of her. She scooped up a small portion and offered them to Kimberly. "You?" From her tone Grant got the impression that she didn't really want to know.

"I feel great." Knowing Tracey shared the same physical desire, even if she wasn't ready to admit as much, had somewhat changed his entire perspective.

"Good." With a sudden movement, Tracey got to her feet and opened the refrigerator door, then peered inside. She retrieved a pitcher of orange juice and poured some in a small glass.

When she spoke again, she jumped right into her plans for the day. "I checked on Stephanie, and she's still sleeping. I have an appointment at nine with my eye doctor today, but I can break it if you want me to go with you when you take her to see her pediatrician," she said, keeping her back to him.

"Thanks for offering, but I can take her. Are your eyes bothering you?"

"No. I'm getting contacts. I'm tired of wearing glasses." She turned toward him to demonstrate her frustration, giving her glasses a little nudge upward. Then, as if she'd realized she'd faced him without meaning to, she quickly looked away. The noticeable tremor of her voice was a dead giveaway that she was far from calm.

"Oh," Grant said, detailing her motions with his

eyes as she lifted the cup of juice to her mouth. Grant took her uneasy manner as a good sign. If she hadn't gotten over what happened between them last night it must have meant *something* to her.

But Grant didn't like the way she was trying to keep him at a distance. The tension between them wrapped itself around him and squeeze his heart like a vise.

"Mom will be here any minute." She glanced anxiously at the clock as if her very life depended on the minutes ticking away. "She's going to stay with the girls while I go to the eye doctor. I figure you'll want to leave Kimberly with her while you take Stephanie in."

Grant nodded. The polite conversation they were having was beginning to grate on his nerves. She was acting like a total stranger. He didn't intend to let her get away with it.

Because she could avoid him no longer, Tracey chanced a quick glance at Grant. He was dressed in jeans and a pullover navy shirt. Sitting back comfortably in the chair, he looked calm and totally at ease. And Tracey felt as if she'd committed the crime of the century!

Tracey got a damp cloth from the sink and began to wipe the kitchen table clean, doing anything to avoid actually facing him.

"Sit down, Trace, we need to talk."

Grant's tone sounded demanding. Whether he meant it to, she didn't know. She assumed he did because he didn't apologize.

"I really don't have time right now," she replied without even looking at him, tossing the cloth in the sink and wiping her hands on a towel. "I need to shower and dress. Keep an eye on Kimmie until Mom gets here, please.'' She rushed by him, but was brought up short by his hand grasping her arm, hauling her back beside him.

''Trace—''

''Don't touch me!'' she snapped, losing her composure and hating herself for it. Her eyes momentarily found his and dared him to cross her. He let go of her arm. Her words had accomplished their desired effect.

However, Tracey felt only a moment's relief when he sprang from the chair and confronted her, his large body blocking her path of escape.

''Look, I don't know about you, but I don't like the way we're dancing around each other.'' When she didn't respond, he raised his voice. ''Tracey, look at me!''

Instantly Tracey's gaze flew to his, and she glared up at him. Whatever had happened between them, it didn't give him the right to bully her. Gritting her teeth, she faced him, her brown eyes shooting white-hot sparks.

''That's better,'' he said. Her eyes held pure fire as she gave him her attention. ''And you didn't even disintegrate,'' he added, his tone level.

''I didn't think I would!'' she answered back hotly, her face flushed. He was teasing her now. How he could even joke about it was beyond her.

''Tracey, what happened between us—''

''Meant absolutely nothing,'' she declared, stopping him from saying something she didn't want to hear. ''You want to face the facts? Well, that's it. We were both upset, especially me. My nerves were on edge, and I was exhausted with worry by the time you finally got home.

"I was so relieved Stephanie was going to be all right that I nearly fell apart then and there. It was only natural for you to comfort me, and, well, one thing led to another. It was a trying night, and we both got carried away, that's all." Her lengthy explanation trailed off as he began to glower at her.

"I see you've got it all tied up into a neat little package." Grant closed his eyes for a moment, and Tracey wondered what he was thinking. Anger was in his expression when he looked at her and pinned her with a hard glare.

"Is that how you're allowing yourself to deal with it?" he demanded. "All that mumbo jumbo sounds real nice, but it doesn't really excuse the fact that we were *all over each other*."

"Oh, good grief!" Tracey wailed, sounding affronted. "We've been best friends for years, Grant, and nothing like that has ever happened between us before!"

"Oh, no?" he challenged.

"No!"

"What about the night you turned sixteen?" They were nearly nose to nose, their voices well above conversation level.

Tracey paled, then stepped back, trying to control the tremors inside her. "What about it?" she asked, a little breathless.

"You know damn well what I'm referring to," Grant accused.

So he remembered the night he'd first kissed her. Tracey's mind swam with vivid images of that evening, of the way she'd responded to him. She'd been innocent, and from the way he'd kissed her, he'd been far from it. She knew he'd see through it if she chose to deny the memory, but she did her best to make it seem unimportant.

"Nothing happened."

"Because you were young and a virgin," he told her, suggesting something very well would have if he hadn't stopped kissing her when he did.

And because they were just friends. Remembering that he hadn't chosen to pursue a relationship with her still stung. Tracey ignored his comment and asked, "What's this really about?"

Grant swallowed hard. "It's about you and me," he replied.

"I don't think so, Grant. In the past year you haven't let your guard down and allowed yourself to care for another woman for fear of being hurt again. There are reminders of your marriage all over this house, just in case you might forget and take another chance on life."

"What does that have to do with us?"

"I'm not a fool, Grant. I'll bet it's been a long time for you, huh?"

"Last night had nothing to do with anybody but you and me," he said, and his tone was hard. His hungry gaze passed over her body, titillating her in places to add credibility to his words. "We were two consenting adults doing what comes naturally when they want each other."

"I didn't—"

"Oh…yes…you…did." His dark blue gaze sailed into hers, bold and provoking. "And I wanted you, and if that makes you feel uncomfortable, well then, too bad. Last night you were warm and responsive in my arms, making my body ache for yours. All I could think about was devouring every inch of you.''

"Which further proves my point," she insisted, turning away from him before she melted into a puddle right at his feet. It hurt to hear him admit that his feelings for her stemmed from lust instead of love.

While she was still trying to make some sense of it, he came up behind her and put his hands on her shoulders. As usual, he'd come down straight from his shower. She inhaled the intoxicating scent of his aftershave mixed with the fresh smell of the soap he'd washed with. It gave her a light-headed feeling. Or was it because he was touching her?

"You felt it, too, didn't you?" he whispered huskily, pushing harder, as if trying to wrangle a confession from her. She visibly trembled, and the muscles in her neck and shoulders bunched.

"Grant, I don't want to ruin our friendship." She said what had been worrying her all along. It was all she could do not to do something foolish, like turn to him and press her body close to his. How could she even think such a thing when she knew Grant could never really love her?

She was filling in for him, doing most of what a wife and mother would do, without causing him the pain. She wasn't going to hand over her body, too.

Grant's hands slid down her arms and caught them in a hard grasp. "Nothing's going to happen between us that you don't really want." What was essentially reassurance came out sounding like a seductive promise.

"*Nothing* is going to happen between us, period," she told him, her voice hard with contention.

Tracey missed having a special man in her life. But

she knew better than to believe that Grant could be that man, even temporarily. And she wouldn't risk losing her friendship with him for anything.

He might want her physically, but he would never love her. Not in the way she *needed* to be loved by him.

Grant started a string of curses, then forced back the remaining oaths at the edge of his tongue. He'd done exactly what he'd wanted to avoid—pushed her into a corner where she was ready to fight what she was feeling for him. Last night he'd thought it wouldn't hurt to give her some breathing space. Well, he'd made a big mistake and now he had to figure out what to do about it.

"Tracey—" A knock sounded at the front door, interrupting him. His hands tightened for a brief moment, then he let them fall. Tracey went to let her mother in.

"Hi, Mom. Come on in." Tracey stepped back, and Helen Collins walked into the room with her usual bright smile. She was slightly shorter than her daughter and just a little heavier, yet there was a striking resemblance between the two women.

"Good morning," she said as she and Tracey walked back into the kitchen. She looked fondly at the baby, who was entertaining herself with a toy attached to the tray of her high chair. Kimberly grinned and held out her arms. "And how's my little one today?" Helen unhooked the baby and lifted her into her arms.

Tracey's eyes were evasive, her carriage stiff. Grant had moved to lean against the counter, his legs crossed at the ankle, his hands on his hips. Though he spared Helen a brief smile, his piercing stare was on Tracey.

"I'm a little early. I hope I'm not interrupting anything." Helen's glance flitted between them.

"Of course not, Mom. Thanks for coming." Grant walked over and put his arm around her. Helen Collins was truly the only mother he'd known, because his own mother had died when he was so young. Most of Grant's thoughts of her were little bits and pieces of memories. He remembered she'd smelled like roses and she always hugged him tight and kissed his cheek before he left for school.

And he remembered the pain he'd felt the day he'd come home from school and found out she'd died. He'd told himself that he would never let himself forget how much that hurt.

Growing up, he'd spent more time at the Collins' home than he had at his own house. Bill Collins had always treated him like a son, especially after Grant's father had died during Grant's first year in college.

Helen eyed her daughter. "I thought you had an appointment to have your eyes checked this morning?"

"Um, I do—at nine," Tracey answered.

"Then you'd better hurry or you'll be late." Glancing at her daughter's sweats, she said, "You weren't planning on going like that, were you?"

"No, no I wasn't." Grateful for the reprieve, Tracey forced a brief smile, then headed to her room and dressed in a pair of black cotton twill pants and a cream-colored sweater.

She couldn't forget what Grant had said to her. But he was wrong. Last night Grant had wanted, *needed* a woman, and she'd conveniently fitted the bill. Traumatic experiences often made people do and say crazy things, things they sometimes later regretted.

Though Tracey wanted to believe her own explanation, the memory of lying beneath Grant, his mouth hard and hot on hers, came flooding back, making her head swim, her body ache. Just as he'd said, she'd been on fire for him, had wanted him to make love to her.

For a few wonderful, heady minutes, she'd allowed herself the pleasure of loving Grant. She looked at her bright red cheeks in the bedroom mirror and faced the sadness that crept into her eyes. How would she ever forget?

When Tracey arrived back in the kitchen, Stephanie was up and sitting at the table. She looked perfectly normal, not at all like the sick child she'd been last night.

Tracey glanced at Grant and found him watching her. She turned toward her mother. "I shouldn't be gone more than an hour."

"Take your time. Why don't you take it easy today since I planned on being here—maybe do some shopping or get that haircut you've been putting off," Helen suggested.

"I don't want to take advantage of your time."

"Don't be silly. I've nothing else planned for the morning."

Tracey smiled. "Maybe not, but you and Dad are already sitting tonight so Grant and I can attend his company's party." Grant had asked her to go with him when his company announced the charity event. Tracey wondered now if it was a good idea. Maybe they needed some breathing space.

"We're more than happy to do it," Helen responded.

"Okay," Tracey finally agreed. She picked up her purse and fished her keys from the inside pocket. Tracey always kissed the girls goodbye before she left, so she knew Stephanie was expecting her to do so. However, Grant was now holding his daughter, and Tracey wanted to avoid getting close to him.

Trying her best to appear at ease, she gave Kimmie a quick peck and slowly walked over to where Grant was leaning his back against the range. She bent forward, and Stephanie met her halfway with a loud, smacking kiss. Before Tracey could move away, Grant quickly pressed his warm lips against her cheek. Startled, Tracey lifted her gaze to his.

"I'm sorry," was all he said. His expression was solemn, his eyes shuttered.

Tracey knew what he meant. Apparently some of what she'd said to Grant had made sense, and he now believed that last night had been a mistake. She hoped he also believed that they should put the intimate scene between them in the past and go back to being best friends once again.

"Oh, Grant," she whispered huskily, unable to suppress the grateful smile that came to her lips. She was eager to share the easy rapport they'd always had, and her eyes filled with appreciation because he'd taken a big step in accomplishing that.

"See you later," she said as she left the room, giving her mother a wave as she walked out the door.

Her exam went well at the optometrist's office, and the doctor prescribed the lenses she needed. As she left, she marveled at how it felt to go without glasses.

Afterward she stopped by the beauty salon for the hair trim she'd been meaning to get.

Tracey also decided to shop for a new evening dress to wear to the party. She found a gown on sale at a specialty shop that she frequented. The midnight-blue dress was both elegant and provocative. After purchasing heels to match, she checked her watch and was surprised at how much time had passed.

On the way back to Grant's, Tracey found herself wondering what he'd think about her new dress and whether he'd think she looked sexy in it. Then she admonished herself. She had to get back to thinking of Grant as her best friend and nothing more. She'd mastered that ability perfectly for years.

Until last night, her mind taunted as she pulled into the driveway of Grant's house.

Tracey rushed in the front door, the dress she'd purchased hanging over her arm and the other package clutched tightly in her hands. She dumped the shopping bags in a chair and draped the dress over the back of it before heading for the kitchen.

"Mom, you're a godsend!" she exclaimed with a smile as she walked in and saw her mother and the girls. "You wouldn't believe how much I got done."

"Tracey, Tracey, look what I got!" Stephanie, vying for attention, held a small object in her hand and waved it in the air like a trophy.

"She has to use an inhaler?" Tracey asked, a little panic in her voice. "I thought she'd just have to take medicine." She stood up and went to Stephanie's side.

"Only when she has trouble breathing. She also has medicine to take," Helen said. "Eventually she'll have to be tested to see what she's allergic to. She's not too crazy about getting shots, but Grant said she was a brave little girl.''

A knot formed in Tracey's stomach, and she touched Stephanie's cheek. ''I'm so proud of you.''

''How was your checkup? Any problems?'' Helen asked.

''No, none at all. Look, no glasses,'' Tracey answered, beaming. She turned her attention to Kimberly and was just in time to save a small plastic plate from going over the edge of the tray of the high chair.

''And I took your advice. I got my hair cut, and I bought a new dress. Let me show you.'' Tracey left but was back in the room in a matter of moments, her fatigue apparently forgotten. ''What do you think?'' She held the dress up and pulled off the plastic cover.

''Honey, it's beautiful,'' Helen said, admiring the deep-blue color and the smooth texture of the cloth. ''You're certainly going to look lovely in this. Grant will be with the prettiest woman there.''

''Thanks, Mom,'' Tracey replied, smiling.

Helen reached for her purse. ''Well, I'd better be going.''

''Thanks for staying with the girls, Mom.'' Tracey picked up Kimberly and walked her mother to the front door, Stephanie following close behind. ''I'll see you tonight at seven.'' She watched her mother drive away, wishing she could have talked about what had happened between her and Grant.

But how could she explain that each time she looked into Grant's blue eyes, her heart beat a little faster? Tracey had to do something to put her love for Grant to rest.

Just thinking about the way she'd responded to him started a warm glow in the region of her womanhood.

The glow turned into an incredible ache as the memory sharpened into a picture of the two of them lying in each other's arms.

The guilt Tracey felt was twofold and overwhelming. She'd betrayed her friendship with Grant, and she'd never responded with such sweet abandon to any other man. Not even Richard.

Five

Grant turned the corner, and his heart hammered as he pulled into the driveway of his house. He felt immediate relief when he saw Tracey's car. He'd half expected to find Helen with his children.

He'd asked Tracey a while back to attend a company party with him tonight. After what had taken place last night and this morning, he'd expected her to refuse to go with him.

She was at the sink rinsing dishes when he entered the kitchen, and to Grant she looked beautiful.

"Hi," he said easily, breezing in the door. He glanced at his watch as he put his briefcase on the table. "Sorry I'm late."

She was still dressed as she was when she'd left this morning. He hoped that meant that she just hadn't had time to get ready. He gave her a slow, natural grin, hoping to win back the easy rapport they usually shared.

"Hi, yourself," she replied, giving him a very brief smile. She moved around the kitchen, busying herself. "Mom made a casserole for the girls' dinner while she was here. All I had to do was heat it up for them."

"Your Mom's the greatest," Grant agreed. He sank into a chair near her, so she'd have to look at him when she turned around.

Grant followed her movements with his gaze and tried not to let his mind wander. It didn't work. Her sweater molded her breasts, and her pants hugged her firm tush. Feeling like a sex-starved maniac, he straightened in his seat.

Tracey eyed him cautiously as she stacked dirty plates in the dishwasher. She avoided touching him as she moved around his chair to get a towel to dry her hands.

"Do you want something to drink?" she asked, reaching for a glass in the cabinet.

"You don't have to wait on me, Trace," Grant said. She took care of his kids when he wasn't there. He didn't want her to think she had to take care of him, too. He wasn't a child. He was a man, and he wanted Tracey to think of him as such.

"I don't mind." She put ice in the glass, then retrieved a pitcher of tea from the refrigerator. After filling the glass, she handed it to him. She did it all without looking into his eyes.

"Are we still on for tonight?" Grant asked, hoping she hadn't changed her mind about going.

"I guess. If you still want me to go with you." She sounded unsure.

"Of course I do," he replied.

"Well, since you're home, I'm going to shower and change. Mom and Dad will be here by seven to watch the girls."

"Sure, go ahead. I'll go play with them, then get my shower after you're finished." Grant's gaze slid to the dress hanging over the back of a chair. "Hey, what's this?"

"I went shopping today. I didn't really need a new dress, but you know how I love clothes. This was on sale."

Grant wiggled his eyebrows. "I can't wait to see you in it."

Dead silence fell between them as Tracey's gaze finally clashed with Grant's. He didn't intend to play games with her. He wasn't going to purposely make her feel uncomfortable, but he intended to use every opportunity he could to remind her of the pleasure he'd felt when he'd made love to her. Maybe she wasn't ready to accept what was happening between them, but he was.

Tracey backed up a step, and her cheeks turned pink. "Well, um, I guess I'd better get going if we're going to leave on time."

The atmosphere between them crackled. Grant thought she had to know what he was thinking—that he wanted to pull her into his embrace and kiss her. Everywhere.

All day long he'd tried to tell himself that asking Tracey to marry him and go with him to Atlanta was wrong. But he couldn't quit thinking about it. And he couldn't quit thinking about making love to her.

Grant reached out to take her hand, but stopped when Stephanie, who had wandered into the kitchen and heard their conversation, burst into tears and raced toward Tracey, throwing her arms around her legs and burying her face against her thighs.

"I don't want you to go!" she sobbed.

"Honey, we're only going to be gone for the evening. Grandma and Pop are going to be here with you." Tracey's heart swelled with compassion as big tears slid down her little cheeks. She was concerned about Stephanie getting too excited. "Stephanie," she pleaded, "calm down, sweetheart."

"Stephanie, come here," Grant told her. But the little girl ignored her father, and her crying rose a pitch higher. Cursing under his breath, he barked, "Stephanie!" He got up and reached for her. She clung to Tracey in desperation.

Grant pried her loose and picked her up in his arms. "Hush." She pushed at her father's chest and tried to get free. Grant kept a tight grip on her. "Go on, get ready," he ordered.

"But—" Tracey started to reach for Stephanie.

His blue eyes flashed. "Go get ready. Stephanie will be fine. You can't give in to her."

Tracey snatched up her dress and fled the room before she said something she would regret. She collected her other purchases on the way to her bedroom. Grant had no right to be irritated with her! So his children depended on her, loved her, wanted her with them. Was that her fault? Absolutely not, she fumed, stalking into the bathroom to shower.

The steaming water worked magic on her tense muscles, and the fire slowly went out of her. She felt as if she'd lived a lifetime in the past two days.

She'd known the girls were becoming quite attached to her. It was natural for Stephanie to need mothering when she wasn't feeling well. She was only four years old, too young to understand that Tracey couldn't always be with her. As Tracey patted her face dry with a towel, she resolved to talk to Grant.

She put a hand to her head, realizing that she was working at cross-purposes. She wanted to be there for Grant. Any time, anyplace. Yet she wanted something else, a life of her own, a husband who would give her his heart, a baby. She touched her fingers to her forehead. Just thinking about everything gave her a headache.

She slipped on her new dress and tugged at the fabric until the folds of the dress fell around her legs. It hugged her breasts and hips, and the slit on the side showed a tempting portion of her thigh.

By the time she finished getting ready, Tracey was still confused about her place in this home. Perhaps she'd been a crutch for Grant.

The thought of Grant loving another woman caused momentary panic in Tracey's heart. *You shouldn't be feeling like this,* her conscience reminded her. *He wasn't meant to be yours.*

She told herself she was overreacting,. Her protective feelings toward Grant stemmed from her loyalty to him and from being his friend. For a moment in time she'd let her guard slip and had done something totally irrational. That was all.

Finished dressing, Tracey paused before the dresser mirror and studied her reflection. Her satin dress molded her body, making her feel more like a desirable woman than she'd felt in years. She'd blown her hair dry, and it fell in soft brown and golden waves that framed her face. She smiled at herself, her eyes wide and expressive.

''You look beautiful.''

Startled by Grant's voice, Tracey whirled and faced him. He stood at the door watching her, his gaze roaming over every inch of her, moving slowly from her face, pausing lingeringly at her breasts and continuing down her body to her ankles. It singed every inch of her, making her feel as if she were suddenly on fire.

Every nerve ending seemed to come to life at that very moment, sending a sensual message to her brain. She felt light-headed and woozy.

"Thank...you," she stammered. Her body trembled. He was looking at her as if he'd never seen her before.

Grant shifted away from the door frame and approached Tracey with calculated steps, feeling much like a lion about to claim his mate. His heart felt as if it was going to pound a hole right through his chest. The dress she wore exposed every curve of her luscious body.

"I'm sorry for being so abrupt earlier," he said, his voice whisper soft. The friendship between them was a strong bond. It was going to be difficult to get Tracey to see beyond it and accept him on an intimate level.

He'd begun to think more about asking Tracey to marry him and move to Atlanta, knowing that she was the only solution he had if he was going to be able to take the promotion.

He wasn't thinking totally selfishly in wanting her to mother his girls. He knew how unhappy she'd be if he moved and she wasn't able to see them. Now that he'd made up his mind, he decided to put his plan in action.

He was close enough to her now to reach out and

fumble with a strand of her hair. She drew her head back a fraction. Okay, so she was going to take some convincing. He'd take it slow with her, give her some time to get used to the idea.

"That's all right. I know you've had a long day and you didn't get much sleep last night."

She started to move away from him, but he hemmed her in by placing his hands on each side of her, bracing them against the dresser and standing so close that he knew she could feel his body heat.

"So you got contacts?" he asked, his eyes curiously searching hers. Until that moment she'd avoided looking at him. Like magnets his eyes drew hers until she was forced to look straight into them and face the electricity that sparked between them.

"Uh-huh," she muttered, unable to form a word.

"Your eyes are lovely." So beautiful, the color of expensive whisky, he thought. He watched her tongue wet her lips, and it was all he could do not to groan in agony.

The desire to taste her was too damn strong to resist. Grant's head bent, and he caught her tongue with his lips, kissing it before she could retract it. A bolt of awareness, like white-hot lightning shot through him.

His gaze, hungry and searching, dropped to her breasts, full and soft and round, rapidly rising and falling with her agitated breathing. The dress she wore exposed enough of her satiny flesh to tempt him to forget his plans and take her, right then and there.

Grant lowered his head and touched his lips to the base of her throat, slipping his tongue out and tasting her. Her skin smelled lightly of jasmine, her favorite perfume, and he inhaled deeply, savoring her essence.

Tracey closed her eyes and moaned, and her hands came up against Grant's chest, intending to push him away. Instead, as if she'd lost the power to control them, they slid over his muscled shoulders and around his neck and pulled him closer to her. His breath against her skin tingled as he bestowed soft, tantalizing kisses along her jaw.

When his teeth sank softly into her earlobe, she gasped with pleasure, and it was all the encouragement Grant needed. His hands slid to her hips and tugged her closer as his mouth smothered hers.

Their bodies molded together, fitting perfectly, and heat raged between them. Hot and wild. His tongue plunged into her mouth, seeking and finding hers. They both moaned, consumed by the sudden passion that flared between them.

One of Grant's hands moved from her hip to her thigh, inching her dress up until it was bunched around her bottom. As he explored her mouth, his other hand held her head captive, his fingers splayed through her now disheveled hair.

Tracey lost all sense of time or place or circumstance. Grant's tongue was doing wonderful things, erotic things, to her mouth. She gasped for air when his lips left hers, then sucked in a sharp breath as he kissed his way down her throat. His tongue found and stroked her deep cleavage, and Tracey was sure that time ceased to exist at that moment.

Never before had she experienced such a staggering response to a man. It frightened and excited her at the same time.

When he suddenly pulled back, Tracey opened her eyes and stared up at him, totally stunned and confused. He slowly released her and pulled her arms from around his neck.

"I'll get that," he said, realizing that she hadn't heard the doorbell.

Tracey stared at him. "What?"

"The door," he whispered. His lips curved into a slow, totally wicked smile, and he winked at her. He was pleased she'd forgotten time and place, and considered it a score in his favor.

"It must be your parents." He checked his watch. "They're right on time, and I still need to grab a shower." He got only as far as the bedroom door when he heard her call his name, the husky tone of her voice sounding seductive to his ears. He faced her, his expression giving none of his emotions away.

"Yeah?"

"What…what was that all about? I mean, why did you kiss me like that?"

"Think about it, Trace."

He walked out of the room, and Tracey slowly turned and faced herself in the mirror, aghast at her appearance. She tugged her dress down and did her best to smooth out the wrinkles with her hands.

What did he mean? And what in heaven's name was wrong with her? Though not earth-shattering, the intimacy she and Richard had shared had been… pleasant. Richard could never have been described as romantic.

Tracey put a hand to her head. She shouldn't be comparing Grant to Richard. She'd tried to love Richard. She thought she'd put her feelings for Grant in perspective.

Grant, however, had stirred something deep inside her. The desire that had soared through her body was now like an unsatisfied ache that begged to be fulfilled. Tracey closed her eyes and moaned, telling herself she was losing her mind.

Okay, she admitted to herself, she loved Grant. So what? She'd always loved him.

But Grant doesn't love you, her conscience taunted.

She had to remember that. Living in the same house with him was taking its toll on her. After all, Grant was a very sexy man, and she was only human to notice his virility. Close quarters did that sometimes. Tracey put a hand to her face, trying to cool her hot skin.

What, exactly, was Grant trying to prove? She frowned as she tried to figure out his motives.

She looked at herself in the mirror once again. She wasn't going to be successful getting her relationship with Grant back to the way it was if she continued melting in his arms when he held her.

Change of any kind made Tracey nervous, and the changes taking place between her and Grant made her unsure of her ability to control her life.

Tracey repaired her hair and makeup before walking into the living room a few minutes later, where she found her parents with Kimberly and Stephanie.

"Hi, Mom, Dad. Thanks for coming over. Grant will be back down in a minute. He's getting ready." Her mother was holding the baby. "You're going to spoil her, you know."

"Like you don't," Helen replied, a smile on her lips.

"Guilty," Tracey admitted. "Grant got the girls ready for bed. The number where we'll be is on the table by the phone in the kitchen."

"You look lovely," her mother commented. "I

was right. That color is lovely on you. Isn't it, Grant?''

Grant's gaze slid appreciatively over Tracey as he joined them. ''You look gorgeous,'' he agreed, picking Stephanie up and hugging her. His blue eyes speared Tracey's and she blushed.

''I guess we'd better be going.'' She collected her purse and a light jacket from where she'd laid them when she walked into the room.

Grant gave Stephanie to Bill, then opened the door for Tracey as they said goodbye. She felt his hand against her back and tried not to let the sensation of his nearness affect her.

After handing Tracey into his car, he rounded the front and slipped behind the wheel. Tracey strove to put their relationship back on an even keel by making light conversation. They talked a little about Grant's work and a bit about hers. Tracey described a piece she'd just been asked to complete for a client.

They arrived at the hotel and upon entering saw a sign directing them to the room where the party was taking place. It was an elegant setting. The dimly lit ballroom was decorated in mauve and beige tones, with lit candles on each table.

Grant took Tracey's hand as he moved through the room, stopping along the way to chat with people he knew. He put his arm around her and drew her to his side as he introduced her to the people she hadn't met.

Tracey didn't know exactly what to think. They'd been to several company functions together and never before had Grant acted so possessively. It made her feel warm and secure, yet also uneasy. Grant was behaving as if they were on a real date, and they'd gotten quite a few curious looks from several people.

Grant seemed oblivious to the stares sent their way, but Tracey hadn't missed them. Especially when they ran into his secretary. Melanie's gaze flitted over Tracey. It was obvious that she was curious when she noticed Grant holding Tracey's hand.

"Hi, Grant." Melanie slipped away from her date, who was talking to another couple, and moved closer to Grant. She ran her fingers along his arm, her look seductive.

"Melanie." Grant acknowledged her with a warm smile. "You look beautiful tonight," he commented. He looked toward Tracey and drew her closer to him. "You remember Tracey," he added.

"Of course." Melanie's glance was brief and dismissive. She quickly turned her attention back to Grant, stepping near enough to him to brush her breast against him.

Tracey wasn't stupid, and she knew flirting when she saw it. She'd had a suspicion for a while that Grant's secretary had a thing for him. She didn't know how Grant had missed it. Or maybe he hadn't, she told herself.

Someone began tapping on the microphone to get the crowd's attention. Grant started to move away, but Melanie delayed him by gently grasping his arm.

"Don't forget you promised to save me a dance," she reminded him.

Grant nodded, then ushered Tracey toward their assigned table. Robert Babcock and his wife, Pat, were already seated, and they quickly exchanged greetings. Introductions to other company representatives and their spouses were made as Grant and Tracey took their seats.

The food was excellent, baked chicken served with

a honey sauce and red potatoes. As the evening progressed, Tracey was glad she'd come. She was comfortable with Robert and his wife, as she had known them for some time. She didn't know the other people at the table, but enjoyed their company as well.

After a couple of speeches and a presentation to Robert acknowledging his company's part in raising money to build an animal shelter, the lights were dimmed and the music began. As the band began the third song, Grant took Tracey's hand and tugged her out of her seat and onto the dance floor for a slow tune.

Grant pulled Tracey into his arms, fitting her body against his as he began to move to the music. Tracey gave herself to the moment. It wasn't as if she hadn't danced with Grant before, but this was the first time he'd held her so close with this new awareness between them. Tracey closed her eyes. She felt as if she was warm liquid poured into a human mold.

She was in trouble.

Grant put his chin near her cheek, and his breath fanned her ear. Tracey melted a little more. With a little tightening of his arms, Grant pressed her even closer. Tracey found it hard to believe they could still move their feet.

Over the course of the next hour they danced several times, all of them slow dances. Robert had managed to get Tracey on the dance floor for a fast tune while Grant had gone to talk to one of his assistants.

Tracey was sitting back at the table when she saw Grant making his way toward her. Her heart did a little flip as she realized another song had started, one of her particular favorites. She knew that's why Grant was rushing back, and it made her feel good inside.

He was almost to her when Melanie cut him off and grasped his arm. She drew him closer and whispered into his ear. Tracey watched with disappointment as Grant's eyes connected with hers apologetically, indicating there was nothing he could do.

Well, Tracey knew how he felt because there was nothing she could do about the jealousy she felt as she watched Melanie mold herself against Grant.

Tracey turned in her seat, unable to bear watching Melanie put moves on Grant. Robert wasn't in his chair, and Tracey started making conversation with Pat. After a few moments Pat stunned her by mentioning something about a promotion for Grant.

"What?" Tracey's eyes widened. "Grant hasn't mentioned anything about a promotion," she said, frowning.

Pat immediately looked embarrassed. "Oh, my." She put a hand to her reddened cheek. "I'm sorry. Please don't let on that I said anything," she pleaded. "Robert said it hadn't been announced at work, but I just assumed Grant had talked with you about it."

Confusion formed lines across Tracey's forehead. "He hasn't said a word," she admitted.

"Then obviously I shouldn't have said anything," Pat rushed on. "Robert said Grant was thinking the offer over, that he hadn't made a decision yet."

"But why not?" Tracey asked. "Why wouldn't he want it?"

Pat looked as if she'd said too much already. "There's a lot involved," she said evasively. "Oh, goodness, here comes Robert." Her hands played with her linen napkin. "Please don't say anything," she asked again.

"Of course I won't," Tracey promised as Robert joined them at the table.

Tracey looked on the dance floor for Grant. After a moment she spotted him with Melanie, and a knot formed in her stomach. They were dancing nearly as close as she and Grant had been, and Melanie was using every moment to touch him as intimately as possible. Her hands were on his neck, her face close to his.

At that moment Tracey didn't know which bothered her more. Grant not mentioning the promotion or Melanie's blatant attempt to seduce him.

She took exceptional pleasure when the song ended and Grant walked Melanie to her seat. Tracey's gaze followed his progress as he made his way across the room toward their table and joined her.

"I tried to get back for that song, but—" He shrugged his shoulders as if he'd been helpless.

"That's okay." Tracey realized there was nothing Grant could have done.

"Having fun?" he asked, his eyes searching hers.

"Yes. I'm glad I came," she admitted, and her smile was genuine.

Grant took her hand in his and gently rubbed his thumb over it. "I'm glad, too. I enjoyed dancing with you."

Tracey frowned at him. "You appeared to enjoy dancing with Melanie," she commented, then she wished she'd kept a tight leash on her tongue.

"Melanie?" Grant chuckled. "She's harmless. She likes male attention."

"It looked to me as though she certainly had yours."

Grant smiled seductively. "Jealous?"

Tracey refused to admit the truth. "Why would I be?"

"Why, indeed," he answered, and let go of her hand.

Grant had thought the evening had gone well up to that point. He was with Tracey. She looked gorgeous and he couldn't keep his eyes off her. Or his hands. He touched her at every opportunity. And best of all, he was able to hold her in his arms half the night without letting her know how hard it was not to kiss her.

He was disappointed when she mentioned leaving, but she reminded him that it was late and added that she was tired. They said their good-nights and made their way to Grant's car. When they arrived home, Helen and Bill assured them the children had been fine. After they'd left to go home, Grant turned around from seeing them to the door and was disappointed when he saw Tracey picking up her keys.

"Where are you going?" he asked, knowing she was leaving, but asking, anyway.

"I thought I'd go home for the night." She picked up her purse.

"Why?"

"The girls are all right. I've been over here the past two nights," she told him. "I have to go home sometime."

"Stephanie will be disappointed when you're not here in the morning," he reminded her.

"I can be back before she wakes up." Tracey slipped her light wrap around her shoulders.

"It's late. It makes more sense for you to stay here." Grant didn't want her to go. But he couldn't tell Tracey that. "Besides, I don't like the idea of your being out alone so late at night."

"Grant, I've gone home this late before." Tracey moved toward the door. "I'll be back early," she promised.

Grant walked her to the door. "I wish you'd change your mind," he said, trying one last time to convince her.

Tracey faced him. Her eyes held his.

"I need to go home," she insisted. "But I want you to call me if you need me during the night. I mean, you know, if Stephanie wakes up and is ill," she qualified.

"She'll be okay," he said. *I won't, though,* he thought. Grant still wished she'd stay the night. Even if he couldn't sleep with her, he liked having her in his house.

Tracey's eyes connected with his, her look serious. "If she isn't, I want you to call me," she insisted. "Promise?"

Grant agreed, then followed her to the door. She didn't resist when Grant hugged her to him, and he was glad of that. He'd wanted to hold her one more time. He wanted to do a lot more than hold her.

"Thanks for going with me."

"I had a good time," she whispered. "I'll see you in the morning." Tracey moved out of his arms and opened the door. She had to leave before he talked her out of it.

Six

The telephone ringing in the dead of the night was like the alarm at a fire station, startling Tracey out of a deep sleep. She groped for the receiver and pressed it to her ear.

"Hello," she murmured, her voice husky.

"Trace, it's Grant."

Tracey forced her eyes open and looked at the clock. It was the middle of the night. She became worried when she heard Stephanie's cries in the background.

"What's wrong?" she asked, her voice anxious.

"Stephanie woke up. She was having trouble breathing. I gave her medicine. She's feeling a little better, but she keeps asking for you."

"I'll be right over," Tracey said quickly. "I just need to throw some clothes on."

"I'm sorry, Trace."

"Don't be. I wanted you to call," she insisted. "I'll be there within ten minutes."

After she hung up the telephone, Tracey jumped out of her bed and pulled on a pair of jeans and a beige shirt that buttoned up the front. Instead of stopping to put in her contacts, she carried them with her and wore her glasses. When she arrived at Grant's, he was waiting for her at the door.

"Thanks for coming," he said gratefully, and looked relieved to see her.

"Grant, don't worry about it." Tracey shrugged out of her jacket and asked, "Where's Stephanie?"

"I finally got her in bed." He looked as tired as Tracey felt. "She wore herself out, I think." He waited for her to go ahead of him, then followed her down the hallway.

The door to Stephanie's room was slightly ajar, and Tracey could hear quiet whimpering coming from inside. She peeked in, letting her eyes adjust to the dim night-light casting a soft glow on the room.

What she saw tore at her heart. Stephanie was curled into a little ball, her thumb stuck in her mouth. Tracey remembered the exact day that Stephanie had pronounced herself too old to suck her thumb. She'd been so proud of herself. That she was reverting to habits of insecurity wasn't a good sign.

Tracey walked softly into the room and stopped beside Stephanie's bed. The little girl sensed her presence and opened her eyes. With a faint whimper, she raised her arms and called out Tracey's name. Tracey sat on the edge of the bed and gathered the small one into her arms, brushing her hand over her dark head with soothing strokes.

"Hush, sweetheart, Tracey's here," she murmured.

Stephanie clung to her. Tracey glanced at Grant, who was watching them from the doorway.

"Hush now," she cooed. Her eyes met Grant's in the shadows. The pain she saw in them racked her body with emotions she couldn't even name. "Honey, don't cry anymore. I'm going to hold you until you fall asleep," she whispered.

Stephanie sniffed, and Tracey wiped the child's nose with a tissue from her pocket.

Grant watched Tracey stretch out beside his daughter. His heart ached for both of them. Tracey was a beautiful and compassionate woman, with enough love in her heart for a dozen children.

He thought again about asking Tracey to marry him. Grant knew how selfish it was to offer her marriage without a chance for children of her own, but he didn't know what else to do. He already had two children. He didn't want more. Maybe his girls would be family enough for Tracey to agree to marry him. He could only hope.

Later, in his room, Grant lay on his bed with his hands beneath his head, his eyes fixed on the ceiling. He felt exhausted, as if he'd been to hell and back. Every muscle in his back and neck ached from the tension and strain pulling at him.

Tomorrow he was going to ask Tracey to marry him.

The next morning, showered and dressed, Grant went in search of Tracey to talk to her. He found her in her workroom, working on a small angel. She looked like an angel herself, dressed in white slacks and a shirt made of blue denim. Her hair was pulled up behind her head with a barrette. Some of it had escaped and framed her face.

Grant stopped on his way into the room to speak to Kimberly, who was in her playpen beside Tracey.

"Hey," Tracey said, as he straightened from kneeling and talking to the baby. "What time is your flight?"

"It leaves around twelve-thirty."

"Do you need a ride to the airport?" she asked, taking in his casual attire. Grant had put on jeans, a white shirt and sneakers. He was so handsome, and Tracey's heart did a little flip when her eyes roamed over him. Quickly, she glanced down at her work.

"No, I'll park in the long-term lot and leave my car." He came farther into the room and stopped beside her. "Trace, there's something I need to talk to you about."

Tracey looked up.

"Where's Stephanie?" Grant asked.

"In the playroom," she answered, turning in her seat to look at him. His serious expression surprised her. She wondered what had him tied up in knots.

"Are you busy?" he asked, his eyes searching hers.

"Nothing that can't wait. What is it?" she asked.

"Let's go into the den where we'll be more comfortable," he suggested.

Tracey nodded and got out of her seat, glancing at Kimberly to make sure she was all right. She bypassed the den where Grant had almost made love to her and went into the living room.

He waited for her to sit down, but instead, she stood beside the large, blue, contemporary recliner. Grant sat on the matching sofa. He leaned back and struck a nonthreatening pose, crossing a foot over his knee. "I want to talk about what's happening between us," he stated bluntly.

Surprised flashed across Tracey's features, and she quickly made an effort to stop the conversation before it got started. "I don't. I told you that." She hadn't expected Grant to force the issue.

"Tracey, we almost made love a couple of nights ago."

"Grant, please—" Tracey wanted to block out his words of seduction, words that made her feel as if a mind-altering drug had been injected into her veins. The husky sound of his voice flowed through her like hot lava from an active volcano, melting her bones and making her feel weak all over. She shook her head in denial. "That never should have happened."

"I know," he answered. The coil of sexual tension in his body seemed to be a controlling force within him. For a year the absence of sex in his life hadn't been a problem.

Now his body was rebelling. He wanted a woman—badly. And not just any woman; he wanted Tracey. He wanted to taste her sweet lips, wanted to kiss every inch of her smooth, delectable skin, wanted to lose himself in the feel of her mouth under his, her body writhing beneath him. His hands ached to touch every inch of her, and he had to steel himself from going over to her right now and showing her just what she was doing to him.

Grant sat forward as he began to speak. "Tracey, I gave my marriage everything I had to give. I trusted Lisa, and even when I suspected she was fooling around, I stayed, hoping we could work things out.

"But as much as I hate to admit it, I need a woman

in my life.'' Lines of tension formed across his fore-head. ''I don't mean to sound crude, but I'm a man—a living, breathing man—and I have needs.''

Tracey looked at him and her expression was guarded. ''I've encouraged you to start dating again.''

He was so handsome, with his devilish grin and twinkling blue eyes. Her heart throbbed with jealousy. It ate at her, silently consuming every part of her body.

''Yeah, I know, and I've given it a lot of thought recently,'' he admitted. ''I'll admit you were right about the girls needing a mother. I guess it's time I accept that and do something about it.''

Tracey braced herself for what was coming next. He was going to tell her that he'd met someone, or that he was seeing Melanie. *Oh, God.* Pain, sharp and piercing, shot through her, robbing her of breath. Her feelings for him had been at the forefront of her emotions so much lately that she was afraid she'd break down and cry right in front of him.

Grant watched her closely as he began to speak. ''I never thought I'd say this, but I do want to marry again. I'm tired of living alone, tired of not having someone to share my life with, tired of sleeping alone.'' He waited for her gaze to meet his.

''Trace, I want you to marry me.''

Anger flamed through her as she glared at him. ''How can you joke around at a time like this!'' The harsh retort was out before she could stop it, before she was aware of Grant's serious expression. She realized then that he wasn't joking.

Tracey leaned against the recliner, feeling as if a ten-ton anvil had fallen on her. Her stunned silence left an opening for Grant, and he took that opportunity to continue, explaining exactly what he meant.

"It's not such a weird idea if you think about it, Trace. You've always wanted children. When we were young, all you used to talk about was raising a family of your own. You wanted a marriage just like your mom and dad's."

"You're serious!"

"Did you think I wasn't?"

"I don't know what to think," she replied, her voice slightly breathless. His proposal had staggered her. She was finding the entire conversation quite unbelievable. Tracey's heart began to pound joyously. Did she dare hope that Grant was in love with her?

"Just think about what this can mean for all of us. I know raising my children wouldn't be quite the same as mothering your own, but it'll be the next best thing. I know how much you love them, and they both love you so much.

"Kimmie never knew her mother. Stephanie has no real connection with Lisa. For all intents and purposes, you'll be the only mother the girls will ever know."

Tracey realized at that moment exactly what Grant was proposing, and her heart sank. His offer caused a stinging sensation in her chest, and she felt as if a sharp blade had been inserted into her.

"You mean...you mean, you'd marry me to give the girls a mother?" Tracey was flabbergasted. Why would he do that? It had only been a year since his marriage had broken up. Grant didn't have to rush into a meaningless, convenient marriage. He had plenty of time to fall in love again.

"Yes," he admitted honestly. "I've given it a lot

of thought. I'm doing okay with them, but we both know a mother is what's missing in their life. It tore my heart out to see Stef clinging to her blanket last night, crying for you.''

Tracey's mind was whirling faster than the tornado that struck Kansas and sent Dorothy in search of the mighty wizard. ''I...um, I don't know what to say.''

''Say yes. The girls need you. I need you, too.''

''But we've been friends for years,'' she protested, trying very hard to absorb his arguments.

''Best friends,'' he corrected, his eyes darkening, his lids lowering slightly as he studied her. ''Don't you see? We'd have something more going for us than most couples who fall in love. We know each other's likes and dislikes. We get along great and genuinely care about each other. We practically live together, anyway. Why not take it one step further?''

When she started to speak, he forestalled her and continued, ''Don't say anything yet. There's something else you need to know. Robert's offered me a position as vice president with the company.''

She smiled at him. ''I heard about your promotion last night, but not that you'd been offered a vice presidency. Oh, Grant, that's wonderful!'' she whispered.

Grant looked surprised. ''You heard about it last night?''

''Well, Pat said something, then realized she shouldn't have when she found out you hadn't told me.''

''Why didn't you ask me about it then?'' Grant asked.

Tracey shrugged, not letting him know how disappointed she'd been to learn of the promotion from

Pat. "She asked me not to say anything until you told me."

"I see." Grant thought about that a moment. "I didn't tell you because there's a lot to consider. I needed some time to sort it out."

"I understand."

"The good thing about it is that it would cut down considerably on my traveling and give me more time to spend with the girls. And you, too, if you marry me." He studied her for a silent moment, then said, "I want to be totally honest with you. There are some other things to think about."

Tracey held her breath. "What else?"

"This is a pretty big consideration." He hesitated and Tracey wondered what was coming next. "The job is in Atlanta, which means we'd have to move. Now, think about it," he implored, before she could say anything. "I know how much you hate change, but this could be so good for us."

"Is the company expanding?" she asked.

"No. Jim McLaney, who's in charge of the Atlanta office, is taking an early retirement. Robert offered me his job. I'd pretty much decided to turn it down, until I thought of this solution. I didn't want to upset the girls' routine. They've had a pretty rough year, and I can't put them through any more, emotionally." He pulled himself upright and strolled over to her. "And I had to think about you."

"What about me?" Tracey asked, barely finding her voice.

"You stepped in and cared for the girls when my marriage fell apart. Kimberly and Stephanie have formed an attachment to you. I don't have the heart to separate them from the only family they know."

"And you want me to go with you to Atlanta? As your wife?" The words seemed unreal even as she said them.

"I would turn down the job if it meant separating the girls from you."

Tracey couldn't believe her ears. "You would?"

"Of course. I want this promotion, but not at the risk of hurting my children. I want them to have more than I did growing up. I want them to have two parents who love them."

Suddenly it made sense to Tracey why Grant hadn't said anything earlier to her about his promotion. It must have weighed heavily on him to realize that everything he'd worked for was being offered to him, but that he might have to turn it down.

"Don't you think marriage is an awfully drastic step?" Tracey asked, trying to reason with him. "I mean, I could just make the move with you and stay until you were settled in, even find you a housekeeper you could depend on."

"And how do you think that would look?" Grant asked, his jaw hardening as his tone changed. "As if we're shacking up, that's how. Do you want the girls to have that stigma attached to them? What's more important is I have more respect for you than that.

"Besides, this job has a lot of responsibility and demands the loyalty and esteem of the people who work under me. How could I ask for their respect if they knew we were living together without the benefit of marriage?"

"I really hadn't thought of that," Tracey admitted.

"It's not just the promotion, Trace, although I'll admit it plays a big part. This would be good for all of us. You'd get the family you've always wanted, and I'd get a wife and a mother for my children.''

He reached up and gently ran his knuckles across her cheek, then cupped the back of her neck, his thumb lazily stroking the tender flesh of her earlobe. ''Does being married to me seem like such a hardship?''

Wide-eyed, Tracey stared back at him. The heat of his hand scored her cheek.

''I already know how much you love the girls. And I realize your work is important. Once we get to Atlanta and settle in, we can interview for a housekeeper. That would give you plenty of time to work.''

Tracey blinked back tears, then swallowed past the huge lump in her throat. She'd always wanted marriage and children. Now it was being offered to her on a silver platter. Though not the conventional way of beginning a family, she'd have the chance to raise two very special little girls.

She couldn't love them more if they were her own flesh and blood. They were a part of Grant, whom she'd loved for most of her life. But he didn't need to know that, did he? She didn't have to admit to something he didn't want from her. He'd made it clear that he still thought of her as his best friend.

Grant's heart twisted when he saw her holding back tears. They still had a couple of hurdles to cross that he hadn't even mentioned yet. He wanted everything in the open between them and tackled the next issue, wishing he felt as if he was winning her over.

''There's more.''

''I think I'd better sit down.'' Tracey's knees were shaking as she went around him and sat on the sofa. He followed and took a seat, too, leaving a little space between them. She lifted her head, signaling that she was ready for him to continue.

"You need to understand that you'll be my wife, Trace, in every sense of the word. I'll expect you to share every aspect of my life, including my bed."

Tracey blushed hotly as their discussion became more personal.

"Does that surprise you, that I'd want to have sex with you? I've been celibate for over a year, Trace, and you're an attractive, sexy woman. What man in his right mind wouldn't want to make love to you?" Astonishment registered in her eyes, and he chuckled. "What? You don't believe that I've been celibate?"

"It's not that I'd think you'd lie about something like that," she told him, sounding unsure despite herself.

"But?" he prompted.

"I don't understand...why. I mean, surely there have been women who—" She let her sentence fade away and shrugged her shoulders, clearly confused and embarrassed.

"Yeah." He shrugged his shoulders. He could have denied it, but she wouldn't have believed him. "It was just different after my divorce. It was like something had been ripped out of me. I came close to taking a couple of women to bed, thinking I would be able to satisfy my physical needs, but I just couldn't go through with it. I didn't want to get involved with anyone."

"And now?" Tracey asked.

"We'll be living together as man and wife, and as such, sex will be a natural extension of that union. I like kissing and touching you, and I've felt the way you respond to me. Personally, I don't think we'll have any problems in that area.''

He was being brutally honest because he wanted to be sure she knew exactly what he was offering. Love wasn't part of the bargain. He wasn't going to offer her something he was incapable of giving.

''There's one more thing,'' he added. He avoided her gaze and took a deep breath. ''I know raising my girls isn't the same as having your own children. But I want you to know that if we marry, I don't want any more children.''

Confusion wrinkled her brow. ''Why not?'' Her voice sounded odd, raspy and unsure. Still, he didn't look at her, but focused his gaze on the coffee table.

''When I married Lisa, I thought we'd live the rest of our lives together. Admittedly, we didn't have a great marriage, but I did my part to make it work.'' His voice drifted away, and his lids came down over his eyes. His face was knotted with tension, as if he was fighting an evil demon that lurked inside him.

He hadn't really talked about his divorce to anyone, not even Tracey. Moisture teased the outer corners of his eyes. When he looked at Tracey, there was a vast emptiness inside him.

''I never thought that she'd drop out of Kimberly's and Stephanie's lives. Granted, I wasn't looking forward to dealing with her, but I knew the girls needed her. It's been hard being both mother and father to them,'' he said, his voice low.

''Oh, Grant.'' Tracey reached toward him and stroked his cheek, and he leaned his cheek into her palm. ''I know it's been difficult,'' she said with understanding as she drew her hand away.

''I never thought I'd live through those first few

weeks, let alone a whole year. I've wanted to give up more times than you could know. The hardest part was accepting that I couldn't. It took me a while to remember I had two little girls depending on me.''

He blinked his eyes in an attempt to clear his thoughts, then looked at Tracey. Huge tears were sliding down her cheeks. He reached out and brushed them away with the pads of his thumbs. "I'm sorry. I know I'm going about this all wrong. What I'm trying to say is, two children are enough responsibility. My hands are full being a good father to them. I don't want any more children.'' He saw the sharp sting of pain flash through her eyes. "This is important to me. I wanted you to know how I feel.''

The room fell silent, and they stared at each other.

"Grant, you haven't—''

"No, but I have to admit that I've thought about it.'' His look was determined. "I have to be sure. Lisa's leaving was hard on Stephanie. I won't put another child through that again. *Ever*,'' he said, remembering the feeling of desertion when his mother had died. He hated that Stephanie was feeling the same kind of abandonment.

"But, Grant, if you marry me, we won't take any chances,'' Tracey insisted. "Don't do anything rash.''

"I'll wait,'' was all he said.

He didn't really trust her not to betray him, Tracey thought, and that hurt her more than he could ever know. She tried not to think about it, but the pain of his words burned her heart.

"Grant, I've always been honest with you. Have you ever once doubted that?'' He shook his head, but Tracey could see that he was wary.

"I promise to always be honest with you. You have my word," she assured him.

"Are you saying that you'll marry me?" He pinned her with his eyes and awaited her answer.

Tracey wanted to say yes so badly. To do so, though, would be to give up the chance of one day having her own baby.

Was she willing to do that? She wasn't even sure she could have children. She and Richard hadn't had any luck and they'd tried for a year. This was her chance for a fulfilling life, what she'd wanted, dreamed of for so long. With just one small word, it could all be hers. She could mother two beautiful children.

Grant's children.

A warm feeling snaked through her body, and she trembled slightly. Her hands were clasped together and resting on her lap. Grant reached for one of them. The spark of awareness when they touched grew to a full-fledged fiery realization that passed between their gazes.

"What's holding you back, Trace? Is it the thought of being intimate with me?" Grant asked bluntly.

Despite her resolve to remain as aloof from her emotions as Grant was, Tracey's face turned red again. "The idea takes some getting used to. This is definitely new ground between us."

Grant moved closer to her, then tugged her onto his lap and settled her snugly against his body. "Give me a chance to convince you that we can make it work." His eyes fell on her mouth as one hand captured the back of her head.

He touched her lips lightly with his finger, running it delicately over their soft texture. "I won't rush you, honey. I'll give you time to get used to my touching you." His lids slid halfway closed, and he moved his mouth closer to hers. Slowly, oh, so slowly, he edged forward.

She waited with bated breath for him to kiss her.

Grant's lips touched hers briefly, then hovered just above hers. His tongue slid out and traced her mouth, tasting the salt of her recent tears, savoring her essence, committing it to his memory.

"I've been a long time without a woman," he whispered, his hot breath fanning her mouth. Tracey's lips parted, and he could feel the warmth of her hand on the back of his neck. "I'll admit that it'll be difficult, but I'll give you some time to think about how good we could be together."

Then he covered her mouth with his. Her lips were petal soft, and Grant felt them tremble beneath his as he ran his tongue beneath the ridge of her upper lip, across the rise of her teeth, then repeated the sensual ritual with her bottom lip. With painfully slow persuasion, he insinuated his tongue between her teeth, and she opened to his gentle seduction.

Tracey accepted the invasion with a tentative touch of her own tongue, then her strokes became bolder, inviting a deeper intimacy. His tongue withdrew, then plunged again, burying itself in her mouth over and over until she relaxed and melted against him.

Tracey hadn't known kissing could be like this. She felt as if her whole body was about to explode into minuscule pieces. She wasn't naive about sex—she'd just never before experienced this kind of wild, uninhibited yearning. Grant's hand cupped her breast, and she felt the sweet torture of his thumb grazing her hardened nipple. Desire, hot and vibrant, shot through her body. She squirmed in his lap, struggling with their position, wanting to turn and press herself against him.

"You taste so good, so sweet," he whispered, his voice thick, guttural. "Feel what you do to me."

Tracey moaned deep in her throat, aware of his arousal against her hip. She wanted to believe his words, but at the back of her mind another thought tugged at her. He'd admitted that it had been a long time since he'd had sex. It was natural that he'd get turned on so easily.

Any woman would get this reaction from him, her mind taunted. Tracey pushed away from him and sucked in a hard breath.

"Wait," she uttered when he would have pulled her back to him. "I can't think rationally when you're kissing me," she confessed, then wished she hadn't admitted as much.

"Don't think, just kiss me. You'll have plenty of time to consider my proposition while I'm gone." He moved his mouth toward hers, and she stiffened in his arms.

Proposition.

Of course, that's exactly what it was, Tracey reminded herself, and her heart sank with the thought. Grant hadn't confessed to loving her, and she couldn't embarrass herself by blurting out that she loved him, that she had always loved him.

She extricated herself from his arms and got up, then moved across the room, her eyes meeting his. "I need some time to think about this, Grant."

"I know it's a lot to consider," he admitted. Grant figured he'd knocked her off balance, and even though he knew she needed time to think about it, he suddenly didn't like leaving town without her answer. Although he'd wrestled with the idea for a few days and she deserved the same consideration, it aggravated him to have to wait for her answer.

"I'll give you as much time as I can. Robert's waiting for me to make a decision," he finally answered, the muscle in his jaw flexing.

"I understand."

He glanced at his watch, realizing how late it was getting. "I guess I should finish packing."

Tracey nodded, then watched him turn and leave.

Seven

Grant snapped his suitcase closed and carried it downstairs, where he went in search of Tracey. He found her in the kitchen. Stephanie and Tracey were in the process of making cookies. Kimberly was in her high chair, banging a rattle against the tray.

"I guess I'd better be going." Grant couldn't exactly put into words what he felt when he walked into the room and saw Tracey with his daughters—as if she belonged there.

Tracey turned toward him. "Oh. Wait." She grabbed a bag from the counter and handed it to Stephanie.

"We made you cookies, Daddy," Stephanie announced, and gave him a proud smile.

"Well, aren't I a lucky guy," Grant remarked, then kissed his daughter. "I'll be back in a couple of days,'' he promised. ''Be good for Tracey while I'm gone.''

Grant nuzzled his younger daughter's cheek, then picked up his suitcase. Tracey followed him to the back door. He opened it, then turned and pulled Tracey against him, arching her back and settling her hips opposite his. They fitted together perfectly, and he liked the way it made him feel inside. Her hands rested on his chest, and he could feel the heat of her palms through his shirt.

''Give me your mouth, Trace,'' he whispered. ''Let me taste you one more time before I go.''

She didn't lean toward him, but Grant saw the eagerness in her eyes as he moved closer. His lips covered hers with gentle force, sealing their mouths together, flesh against flesh, desire burning between them like red-hot coals. His tongue soared past her teeth and met hers in an erotic duel that showed her what he wanted from her in blatant sensual overtures.

''You make me burn inside,'' he whispered, breathing heavily.

''Grant,'' she whispered into his mouth.

''And you make me forget where I am,'' he moaned against her lips, realizing that he had to get moving or he'd miss his flight. He stepped back and let her go. His eyes studied hers for a quiet moment. ''Think about it, Trace. I'll call you later tonight.''

Tracey watched him drive away, aching to tell him what was in her heart. But she knew she never could. Grant had been open and honest with her. His heart was off-limits. He didn't want to love again, thought he was incapable of doing so.

Tracey knew it would be wrong to put the burden of her love on his shoulders. She wondered if she would be able to live with him as his wife, knowing she would never have his heart.

The next few days seemed to crawl by. Tracey tried to concentrate on her work, knowing the deadline for her current project was fast approaching. When she wasn't working, she found herself preoccupied with the decision of whether or not to marry Grant.

True to his promise he called every day he was gone. Their conversations usually consisted of how their time was spent during the day, a little about his job and also how the girls were doing. He never once asked Tracey if she'd given thought to his proposal— or for her answer.

The morning he was due to return Grant called to let Tracey know when he'd be arriving. He couldn't help noticing she sounded elusive. Obviously, he decided, he wasn't going to get the answer he'd been hoping for.

That he felt discouraged was an understatement of earth-shattering proportions. He'd convinced himself that being a mother to his girls would satisfy Tracey's yearning for her own children. She really loved Stephanie and Kimberly, but evidently he'd relied too much on her maternal instincts. Perhaps she considered him the drawback to the offer.

Defeat pulled at him. He had thoroughly enjoyed the time he'd been in Atlanta and had begun to think of the promotion as a done deal. Accepting it would hang on Tracey agreeing to marry him. She was the biggest problem facing him now.

Beside the fact that she held his fate in her hands, Grant knew he couldn't go on being so close to Tracey every day, wanting her to the point of distraction.

He was conscious of how important she was becoming to him and he would have to be careful not to let her get too close. Everything would work out if he kept Tracey in that corner he'd made for her, away from his emotions. He couldn't begin to let his feelings grow deeper.

Had he banked too much on their friendship, her sexual response to him and the fact that she loved his daughters?

When he arrived home, Grant frowned when he noticed Tracey's car wasn't parked in front of his house. He walked in the kitchen door, then proceeded to the living room.

"Tracey," he called out, hoping she was there anyway.

She didn't answer, and he quickly moved through the house, cursing each room he found empty, not liking the disappointment that grew within him with each confirmation that she wasn't there. He stalked to his bedroom, wondering where she was.

She'd known when his flight was due. Apparently she'd had better things to do than to wait for him. Annoyed, he shucked his clothes and headed for his bathroom to shave and shower, slamming the door behind him.

The steam from the hot water seemed to heighten his indignation even as it massaged the tightness in his muscles. By the time he came out of the bathroom, he was beyond being merely irritated.

He stepped into his room, a white towel knotted low around his hips. He stopped dead in his tracks, surprised to see Tracey picking up his clothes.

"You don't have to do that," he told her gruffly, a frown creasing his brow.

Tracey's movements stilled. "I know. I was just keeping myself busy while I was waiting to talk to you." She'd arrived home and heard the water running. She'd puttered around his room waiting for him to finish bathing.

Clouds of steam rolled from behind him as a fierce scowl covered his face. She didn't miss the hardening of his eyes or the muscle flexing in his jaw. Tension knotted in her stomach.

"So talk," he said evenly.

"Don't you want to dress first?" Tracey suggested timorously. Her eyes followed the track of fine black hair down his torso to where it connected to the soft curling hair below his belly.

A lump surged in her throat, threatening to block the passage of air to her lungs. He was so handsome. And she loved him with all her heart. Enough to let him go if he'd changed his mind, she told herself. Enough to marry him for his convenience if he hadn't.

"Not particularly," he answered, aware of her embarrassment.

She turned her back to him and hung his pants in the closet. "I've been thinking about what you suggested. You know, the other day." She turned around, but kept her eyes averted.

"You mean when I asked you to marry me?" he questioned, making clear what they were discussing.

"Yes." Tracey crossed her arms to keep from shaking. He was so much a part of her life, and she didn't want to give him up.

"Have you changed your mind? I mean, you didn't mention it when you called," she explained, sounding braver than she felt. She moved toward the edge of the bed and stopped beside it.

Grant's gaze connected with hers. "I told you to think about it. I didn't bring it up because I didn't want to pressure you."

"Then you haven't changed your mind?" Her look was expectant, giving way to incredulous. Nervously she ran her hands up and down her arms, trying to warm the chill inside her.

"Why would I?" he asked with a shrug of his big shoulders. "I'm getting the best end of the bargain."

Bargain.

Tracey heeded his choice of words. Still, her heart jumped when she realized he hadn't had second thoughts, that he still wanted to marry her.

Grant moved toward her, stopping just short of touching her, yet aching with the need to. "You've decided?"

"Yes." Tracey stared up at him.

Grant's heart stopped beating. "Yes, you've made up your mind, or yes, you'll marry me?" he asked pointedly, running his fingers through his wet hair, then massaging the achy feeling in his neck.

"Yes, I'll marry you."

Grant released his breath as he pulled her into his arms, relief washing over him. He flattened the lower part of her stomach against his hips and hugged her tightly against him. He'd been so scared that she was going to turn him down. His future, the happiness of his children, had depended on her answer. With a finger, he lifted her face.

"You're sure? This is what you want?"

"Yes," she said quietly, then more firmly, "I'm sure."

Grant's attraction to her was automatic, and since he'd already told her how much he wanted her, he made no excuses for his arousal. "I'll try to make you happy," he whispered huskily.

"I already am," Tracey answered, hoping he wouldn't read too much into her words, praying that he couldn't see how much she loved him. "I'll have two beautiful little girls to love," she added. He didn't want her love, and she would never let herself forget that.

Grant's arms tightened around her. He lowered his head, and his lips touched her neck, her cheek, then finally her mouth. "Thank you," he whispered against them.

Tracey gave herself to his kiss, shyly putting her arms around his neck, pressing herself against him. His damp chest wet the front of her blouse. Her nipples hardened against the cloth as their kiss deepened. Grant's tongue was doing wonderful things, entering her mouth, drawing her tongue into a challenging, pleasurable dance, then withdrawing, only to return again with a rush that stole her breath.

Tracey groaned as his hands went to her blouse. Slowly, agonizingly, he unfastened each button and exposed the swells of her breasts above the lacy line of her bra.

"I want to touch you," he rasped. When she didn't protest, he unsnapped the front clasp and caught her fullness in his palms. His thumb grazed one hard-tipped nipple.

He kissed her then, a deep, soul-stirring kiss that vibrated through her. She responded to him, touching his face, breathing in his scent.

His mouth left hers, only to deliver wet, scalding-hot kisses along her neck. Grant brushed her blouse aside with his head, then caught her nipple gently between his teeth, his velvet tongue grazing it and sending a scorching, fiery heat all through her. Her head back, Tracey's hands were in his hair, holding him to her.

"I want you so much," he groaned, feeling as if he were on a rocket and being hurled into space. He bent and picked her up, his towel dropping away, then placed her on the bed, aligning himself beside her. His hands were hot and insistent, aching to know every inch of her smooth, satiny skin. She arched against him in response, and Grant thought he would burst from wanting her.

"Yes," she whispered, nuzzling his clean-shaven cheek.

Grant's mouth returned to hers, devouring her lips, sucking her tongue, tasting her sweet response. He unfastened her jeans, then slowly eased the zipper down. She arched against his palm when he touched her. Her belly was like satin, warm and soft, and he ached to be inside her, to fill her, to feel her surround him, to make her his.

The ringing of the doorbell jarred them both, and Grant jerked his head up, desire raging in his blue eyes. Before he could catch his breath, it rang again.

Cursing, he muttered, "Who the hell is that?"

Tracey eyes widened. "Mom and Dad!" she practically screamed, breathing heavily.

"What?"

"They're bringing the girls home. Stephanie and Kimberly spent the morning with them," she explained hurriedly, suddenly aware that Grant was totally naked.

"I guess we have to let them in." He knew they did—he just didn't want to leave her. He dropped a kiss to one pink-tipped breast and said, "You pull yourself together, and I'll go down and get the door."

Pushing off the bed, he quickly walked to the dresser where, unconcerned by his nudity, he pulled on a pair of dark-blue briefs and some jogging shorts. "Don't be long. We have a lot to tell them." He looked at the desire lingering in her eyes, and it pleasured him to see a soft blush rise in her cheeks.

Tracey nodded and watched him leave, then made a beeline to her bedroom for a clean blouse, thinking of how thoroughly masculine Grant had looked pulling on his shorts. Tall and lithe, with a flat stomach and tight buttocks and strong, powerful legs. She tried to get her mind off how much she wanted to stroke every inch of him.

She quickly ran a brush through her hair, her hand shaking as nerves tingled along her spine. Grant was in the den with her parents, she thought anxiously, telling them God knows what.

By the time she got there, Grant was talking pleasantly with her mother and father. Helen was sitting in the recliner and Bill stood beside her. Grant was across from them on the sofa. Somehow he'd found the time to pull on a T-shirt. His hair was a little mussed, and he looked as if he'd been jogging and had just come in.

Tracey walked across the room and hoped the trembling in her legs didn't show. Bill was holding Stephanie, and Kimberly was sitting on Helen's lap, babbling delightfully. She grinned when Tracey came closer, then raised her little arms, wanting Tracey to pick her up.

Tracey tucked the baby in her arms and sat near

Grant on the sofa. Stephanie promptly scooted out of Bill's arms and was welcomed onto her daddy's lap.

"Hi, Mom, Dad." Tracey greeted them, and wondered if they noticed the strain in her voice. "I hope the girls were good for you."

"They always are," Bill assured his daughter.

"We enjoyed having them." Helen smiled at the two children. "Grant," she asked, "are you going to be in town for a while or are you expected to leave again soon?"

"I'll be here for a few more days, then I'll have to head back to Atlanta."

Helen nodded. "Have you been able to find a new housekeeper?"

Grant glanced at Tracey and cleared his throat, then looked back at her parents. "Funny you should ask. I'm not looking for one anymore," he stated, and waited for the announcement to sink in. "Uh, Tracey and I have something rather important to tell you."

Grant reached over and took Tracey's hand in his. Her skin was cool under his warm palm, and he squeezed her fingers lightly. "We've been doing a lot of talking, about my job and my situation with the girls. You both know how hard it's been for me to keep a housekeeper."

"I've never seen anything like it," Bill commented. "I think you've had a string of bad luck. These children are easy to take care of. You just haven't found the right person yet."

"Actually, I think I have." Grant cleared his throat and said, "This is probably going to come as a shock, but here goes. I've asked Tracey to marry me, and she's accepted. We both hope to have your blessing."

For a few moments the room was utterly quiet. The

faint ticking of the mantel clock seemed more like a drumroll.

"Well," Helen ventured, "I must say that I certainly wasn't expecting this." She didn't look displeased, just sort of shell-shocked by the announcement.

Grant's gaze traveled to Bill. The man had been like a father to him, more so than the man who biologically produced him. Grant's father had never really had time for him.

Bill had been the one to show him how to drive a car and to take him for his permit. He'd been the one to answer Grant's questions about girls.

"I don't want you to worry, Bill," Grant said. "I promise to be good to Tracey."

Bill fixed him with a pensive stare, then turned his gaze on his daughter and said only four words. "Tracey, are you sure?"

She looked directly into her father's eyes, reassuring him she was certain of her decision. "I've always wanted children, and you know how much I love the girls." She didn't admit to loving Grant, and Grant hadn't declared his love for her.

Strange circumstances for a marriage announcement, Grant thought. No doubt both of her parents were aware of the omission. Graciously neither mentioned it.

"Is Tracey going to be my mommy?" Stephanie asked, her blue eyes wide with curiosity.

"Yes, sweetie. Is that okay with you?"

"Oh, yes!" Stephanie exclaimed, jumping down from Grant's lap and throwing her arms around Tracey, nearly squashing Kimberly's little body in the process.

Grant's gaze met Tracey's above Stephanie's head, and he saw the love for his children shine in her eyes. There was a hollow feeling inside him, something akin to jealousy, which he knew was ridiculous. He was asking a lot of her to raise his children. He should be happy that she loved them.

Still, a part of him was a bit annoyed, and he couldn't deny it. It wasn't as if he wanted, or needed, Tracey's love.

He'd put his heart away a long time ago. He never wanted to feel such emptiness again, so it made sense to remember that this union wasn't a love match.

"There's one more thing," he said, his voice steady as he shifted his attention back to Helen and Bill. "I've been offered a promotion at work."

"Well, it certainly seems as if a lot has been happening," Helen commented, still looking quite stunned.

"I don't want you to be upset by this. If I take the job, it means we'll have to relocate to Atlanta." He saw their uneasiness and understood their misgivings. "It's not that far, only a few hours' drive away. You can come and stay with us as often as you want."

"Atlanta!" Helen exclaimed. Her smile wavered on her lips, and she brushed a tear from her eye.

"Grant doesn't mean *if*," Tracey interjected. "He *is* taking the promotion. He's worked hard for it, and he deserves it." Her pride for him showed in her eyes. "He can't relocate to Atlanta by himself, hoping to find the right person to care for the girls. He needs someone dependable to take care of Stephanie and Kimberly, and I couldn't bear to be separated from them. This seems like the right thing to do, Mom and Dad."

She realized she'd as much as admitted that she and Grant were marrying for convenience. Her parents looked disconcerted, but let it go.

"We're happy for you, Grant, and you know how much we care about you. This is just happening so fast," Helen offered.

Tracey shook her head. She understood her parents' reservations. "Grant and I have talked about it for a few days, so we've had more time to get used to the idea. You will, too, as time passes," she assured them both.

Bill sat forward and pinned them both with a curious stare. "Though this is going to take some digesting, I trust you know what you're doing," he began, then focused on Tracey. "Do you still plan to work?"

Tracey was quick to reassure him. "Oh, yes." She'd been thinking about her work while Grant was away. "I can still put some of my things in the local shops here and start working on building my business there." Actually, she was looking forward to the challenge of conquering a new market.

"When are you planning to get married?" Helen asked.

Tracey looked at Grant. They hadn't had time to discuss it.

"As soon as possible. I have to be down there permanently by the end of the month. That doesn't give us much time." He looked at Tracey. "What do you think?"

"My goodness!" Helen interrupted, and her voice rose to a high pitch. "What about the wedding? How can we possibly put it together that fast?" she asked, looking as if he'd asked her to plan a presidential inaugural ball.

Grant left the decision up to Tracey, saying, "I can go ahead of you if you want to put on a fancy wedding."

"I'd prefer to have a quiet ceremony," Tracey answered, and knew it was the right decision. Besides, a big wedding for Grant and her in a church seemed blasphemous. It was best not to begin pretending this was a conventional marriage. Grant didn't love her, at least not like a man should love the woman he was going to marry.

He did care deeply for her, and it had become quite obvious that his passion for her was genuine, for certainly he couldn't fake his reaction to touching and kissing her.

But it didn't mean he couldn't feel the same desire for any other woman, a little voice taunted.

Tracey ignored the inner warning and suggested, "What about having a small ceremony at your house, Mom? I think it would be special to be married in front of the fireplace. We could get a justice of the peace."

"Oh!" Helen's expression brightened and was laced with a new excitement. "Well, anything you want, of course."

"Thanks, Mom. The girls have been through so much this year, and I think it would be best if we move to Atlanta as a family." Glancing his way, she thought she saw relief in Grant's expression.

"Well, Mom, I'm going to have my hands full getting ready for the move. Do you think you can handle the wedding arrangements?"

"I'd love to! Just tell me the date, and I'll get started right away."

After settling on a date that gave them two weeks, everyone stood and seemed to be talking at once as they smiled and hugged each other.

Tracey and Grant stood at the doorway and watched her parents drive off. They seemed to have accepted the news rather well, though Tracey thought her mother was still somewhat dazed, which accounted for why she hadn't put Tracey through the third degree. For this Tracey was truly grateful. She didn't think she would have held up under the strain.

Eight

Later that evening Tracey was resting on the sofa deep in thought. There was so much to consider that she wasn't sure where to start. She made a mental note to call a moving company first thing in the morning. They'd have to transfer things from her apartment as well as everything from Grant's house. It was going to be a nightmare trying to sort it all out.

Grant offered to get them some coffee. When he came back into the room, she had closed her eyes.

"That bad, huh?" Grant asked, moving into the room and handing her one of the mugs before sitting beside her.

"Just a little tired," Tracey admitted, sitting up straighter and sipping the steaming liquid. They sat in silence for a few minutes, savoring the peace and quiet that only came at this time of day.

Finally Tracey asked, "Have you thought about where we're going to live when we get to Atlanta?"

Grant shook his head. "I thought I'd look for something on my next trip down. Do you want to come along? After all, it'll be your house, too."

"No. With so much to do, it would be too difficult to get away. I'll trust you to choose something nice." She couldn't help reminding herself that he should find something *he* liked. After all, it was possible he'd change his mind one day and want out of their marriage.

Right now Grant wasn't looking beyond the present and a quick solution to his problems. Maybe their marriage would work out, maybe not. Tracey would be thankful for each and every day she would have with him.

"If that's what you want," he answered, looking at her with speculation. "We can always move again later if you don't like what I choose." He put his mug down, then slipped his arm around her shoulders as if he'd been doing it all of his life. His fingers slowly brushed the sensitive skin of her neck.

Tracey nodded, marveling at their easygoing conversation, as if their whole lives weren't in the process of metamorphosis. There was a closeness between her and Grant now, which she wasn't really prepared for. During the evening he'd touched her often, caressing her cheek, tugging her to him for a quick kiss, giving her shoulder a gentle rub of reassurance.

Each time she felt his touch, somewhere deep inside a fire smoldered. When Grant kissed her she felt as if the air had been sucked right from her lungs.

It was a little frightening, these new sexual feelings

they shared. She wasn't sure how he would feel about waiting, but Tracey wasn't ready to take that next big step.

"I'm really tired. I think I'll go home." She put her mug on the table and rose.

"Don't go," Grant said, standing and tugging her toward him. She hesitated briefly, then allowed him to pull her closer.

With a finger to her chin, he lifted her face, then planted his mouth on hers, probing her lips, tasting her with his tongue. Though she kissed him back, her response was slow in coming, and Grant felt the pressure of her palms against his chest, the stiffness in her spine. He lifted his head and studied her, looking confused rather than angry.

"Trace—"

"Grant—"

"You first," he said and waited, stroking her back.

Tracey looked up at him and was unable to meet his eyes. She let her gaze drop to his chin. "I think it would be best if we waited." It had been a long day, and she felt totally washed-out. Things were happening in her life too fast; it felt overwhelming. She needed time to herself.

She lifted her gaze to his. Disappointment and frustration showed in his expression. It was obvious that he'd had other thoughts, plans that included picking up where they'd left off earlier when they'd been interrupted by her parents' arrival.

"You do?" He spoke calmly, but Tracey had the feeling he was anything but calm. He leaned away, but his arm stayed around her.

"So much has happened. I think we need a little time to adjust. I mean, this is the house you shared with Lisa. I know it doesn't make sense, especially after this afternoon, but somehow it just doesn't feel right to be with you here.''

Grant moved away from her then, putting a little distance between them. Tracey hadn't meant to hurt him or cause him more pain. She put her hand out to touch him, but his distant expression stopped her.

''I guess I should have thought about how you'd feel, Trace.''

''I'm…sorry—'' she stammered.

''No, you're right,'' he said, cutting her off, his voice sounding strange. ''I should have realized it myself. There are too many memories here. We're starting a new life. We may as well start it right.''

She nodded and looked away, eager to escape his searching gaze. ''I'll come over in the morning,'' she said, picking up her purse and keys from the table by the front door.

Just before she left Grant said, ''I'll miss you until then.''

Grant stood alone in the plush hotel room, listening to the sound of running water behind the closed bathroom door. He paced to the two huge plate-glass windows and pulled back the royal blue curtains, staring into the black night, trying to ease the tension building inside him. He'd managed to keep his libido in check for two very long weeks, and every single moment had been sheer torture.

Only a few hours ago he and Tracey had said their vows. He hadn't known what to expect as he'd waited for her to enter her parents' living room, but he certainly hadn't been prepared for the lovely vision Tracey had made as she'd come to him. She'd literally stolen his breath, and he would remember that moment for the rest of his life.

Her wedding dress, though not elaborate, was of the purest white satin and lace, the bodice hugging her full breasts and small waist, the skirt falling to just about mid-calf.

Feeling undeserving, Grant had repeated the standard promises to Tracey, pledging to love and cherish her. He'd always cared for her in a very special, very personal way. He hoped that through the ensuing years the exceptional bond between them would grow, that she would never regret changing the course of her life for him.

Tracey had recited her marriage vows, her voice sure and strong, yet Grant was aware of her hand shaking as he held it, which told him she wasn't nearly as at ease as she looked. Possibly she had regretted her decision even as she'd said her vows. His heart had turned over at the thought, for they had reached the point of no return.

During their short reception, Helen and Bill announced they had reserved the honeymoon suite for Tracey and Grant at one of the most luxurious hotels in Columbia. Her parents had taken control of the situation and arranged to keep the girls for the night, so Grant and Tracey had accepted their gift graciously.

When Grant heard Tracey turn the shower off, he anxiously looked toward the bathroom door. Then he schooled himself to get a grip. The last thing he wanted to do was to make her uncomfortable. Just imagining her naked in the shower made him shiver with the force of his need to be inside her. The tightening of his body, the throbbing between his legs, made him draw a sharp breath.

The bathroom door opened and swirls of perfumed steam surrounded Tracey as she walked into the room. If Grant had expected her to come to him in a sexy gown, he was to be disappointed. She was wrapped in the fluffy white bathrobe provided by the hotel. An endearing flush ran up her throat to her cheeks as his steady gaze passed over her.

"I'm finished," she told him, eyeing him uneasily as she ran a comb through her wet hair.

Grant gave her a pensive look. Her lips were turned upward with a slight quiver that made him want to reach out and hold her and assure her this awkwardness between them would pass. Instead he paused beside her and gently kissed her cheek, then proceeded to the bathroom and closed the door behind him.

Tracey reached for the hair dryer she'd put on top of the hotel dresser. She glanced around the room as she feathered her hair with her fingertips. A rush of color tinged her cheeks when she looked at the huge bed.

The covers had been turned down, and a single red rose rested on one of the big, soft pillows. There was a bottle of champagne chilling on the nightstand alongside two long-stemmed wineglasses, each adorned with flowing white ribbons—all compliments of the hotel for the honeymooners.

She finished drying her hair and brushed it lightly. She knew the terry robe she wore wasn't exactly alluring. Underneath it all she had on was a snow-white teddy made of the finest silk. She'd purchased it on a whim and was now feeling rather silly about wearing it. It wasn't exactly what a bride would wear when she came to her husband.

Even though theirs wasn't a love match, she wanted to look special when Grant claimed her as his wife. Instead she was feeling inadequate and uneasy. She certainly didn't feel anything close to alluring or sexy. Or like a bride.

Moments later there was total silence in the bathroom, and her heart skipped a beat. She took a deep breath. Grant had been a prince to wait the two weeks she'd asked for. There was no turning back now. It was time to pay the piper.

Despite the fact that when he touched her and kissed her, he made her insides melt, she was still apprehensive about changing this part of their relationship. Tracey couldn't help feeling as if she were burning bridges behind her...bridges that she might need to cross back over someday.

The knob of the bathroom door turned, and her head jerked up as Grant sauntered into the room. He'd slipped his dress pants back on, zipping them up, but leaving them unbuttoned. His hair was damp and fell slightly over his forehead.

Tracey's eyes went to his bare chest and torso, following the whorls of hair that were just as dark as the hair on his head. She averted her eyes, not wanting him to see how much she wanted to reach out and touch him, to test the contours of his rigid muscles. She gave him a tentative smile, every nerve in her body alert.

Grant's gaze stayed on Tracey as he walked over and stopped close to her. His lips curved slightly as his hand lifted her chin, desire burning in his blue eyes. Moving with slow ease, he dropped a brief, tender kiss on her lips.

She pulled back from him, and Grant raised a brow.

"What is it?" he asked gently.

Tracey avoided looking at him. "I think I should warn you."

"Warn me?" Grant repeated.

"I'm not very good at this," she declared, looking away. She'd always felt inadequate with Richard. It was only fair to warn Grant. Not that the damage wasn't done. They were married now. It wasn't as if he could change his mind at this time.

"At what?" he inquired. Then as it dawned on him, he exclaimed, "Do you mean sex?"

Flushing, Tracey finally raised her gaze to his.

"Richard—"

"Let's leave him out of this," he suggested.

Tracey wanted so much to explain that things between them might not be what Grant expected. Just because she enjoyed his kisses, didn't mean he'd be sexually gratified by her.

"But—"

Grant interrupted her by touching her lips with his finger. "No, Trace. Tonight's just for you and me," he assured her. He tugged her closer and nuzzled her hair. "Besides, if what I've experienced so far is an example of not good, then we definitely don't have anything to worry about."

Tracey gave him an unsure smile.

"You smell wonderful," he whispered, touching his mouth to her lips. His tongue slid out and made an undemanding foray into her mouth, then retreated after tasting her.

"You do, too," Tracey answered huskily. His lips

were soft and moist, his body deliciously warm, and she leaned against him, testing his hard-muscled shoulders with her hands. Grant's arms went around her and gently gathered her closer.

"Would you like some champagne?" He snaked a row of hot kisses along her neck to her ear.

"Mmm, no," Tracey whispered, stifling a moan. Liquid fire surged through her, and her legs turned to jelly. Pressing her body against his, she held on to him tightly, feeling as if she'd fall if he let her go.

"You have too much on," Grant told her. His tongue thoroughly caressed the edge of her ear.

"So do you," she answered softly, touching her mouth to the throbbing pulse at the base of his throat. Her hands were pressed flat against his chest, and his skin was hot and damp. Her fingertips caressed the soft mat of dark hair beneath them.

With a groan Grant's mouth claimed hers in a long, seductive kiss. His hands cupped her buttocks, fitting her against him, letting her become aware of his arousal. He had to will himself to go slow with her, when all he wanted was to bury himself in her sweet, slick warmth.

"Grant." She moaned his name, sounding aroused and needful, yet the slight tremor in her voice marked the nervousness she couldn't overcome. Her body trembled in his arms, and he gentled his hold. Even as he wanted to lose himself in her, he felt the need to soothe and reassure her. His hands moved to her throat, and he forced her face up until she looked into the blue fire of desire in his eyes.

"This is a hurdle we have to cross, Trace, if we're going to make this marriage work. I want you. I've made no secret of it." His eyes searched hers, hungry and urgent. "As husband and wife, sex between us is natural and right. Let yourself go with me, honey, and I'll make it good for you. You don't have to be afraid. I'll never hurt you."

Tracey blinked back sudden tears. She wanted this union, ached for it, for she loved him so much. "I know. It's just that it's been so long for me, that I feel as though this is like the first time," she admitted quietly, then dipped her head. "I hope I can please you."

Grant was surprised by her doubts. This wasn't the self-assured woman he knew. He bent to her and tasted her lips, biting them gently, loving them with his tongue. "Just having you in my arms pleases me," he whispered, moving seductively against her. "Sweetheart, can't you feel me?"

She started to speak, but his mouth claimed hers in a hard, blazing kiss that staggered them both. His hands found the opening of her robe and shoved it off her shoulders. It slid freely down her arms and dropped to the floor.

Grant drew away to look at her and caught his breath. Her teddy was silky and sheer, exposing her shoulders and arms and her long, sleek legs. He stepped back and lifted his hand to one of her breasts, gently stroking the tip of it with his finger, watching it bead and pucker under the thin fabric. Continuing to stroke it with his thumb, he fitted the mound of supple flesh to the palm of his hand.

Tracey swayed slightly and one tiny strap fell off her shoulder. Grant eased it farther down, then lifted his hand from her breast and lowered the remaining strap. The garment fell to the floor in a pool when he gave it a slight tug.

She stood before him, naked and vulnerable, and more lovely than he'd ever imagined. She was like a breath of life, and Grant felt his chest swell with a feeling of gratification and wonder. He was a lucky man.

Bending, he lifted her off her feet and kissed her hungrily as he lowered her to the bed. She watched, her eyes half-closed and drowsy with desire as he shed his pants and stretched out beside her.

Deliberate and slow, his fingers traced the contours of her milky-white breasts. Tracey moaned softly, and he swallowed the sound with his mouth, then deepened their kiss, tasting her essence.

Tracey suddenly felt as if she couldn't get close enough to him. She closed her eyes when he looked at her, so afraid he would see how much she loved him, how much she wanted to give the gift of her body to him. She wanted to be perfect for him.

When his mouth closed over the taut peak of her nipple, she gasped, and her eyes flew open, pleasure and longing gripping her fiercely, rocketing the passion threatening to explode inside her. Her body responded by arching sharply against his, and her hands stroked his back and spine.

"Grant." She groaned deep in her throat, her teeth clenched as he tasted and suckled. Fire, liquid and hot, burned between her legs, creating a longing that demanded the kind of fulfillment only this man had the power to give her. His hands were everywhere, touching her intimately, branding her his.

"Please." She begged to be released from this pleasure-pain, to become one with him, to feel the earth move beneath them. Losing a touch of reality, she dug her fingers into his back as she rocked against him, aching for something beyond words, beyond reality.

Dismissing a brief thought about stopping for protection, Grant swiftly moved over her, spreading her thighs wide with his knee. He'd meant to go slow, had wanted to savor every single moment of making love to her, but his need to be inside her was too strong to hold back. He plunged into her with a single hard thrust. She was tight as she gloved him, and it felt so good to be inside her. Like nothing he'd ever known before.

"Trace, oh, honey," he said savagely, his jaw clenched so tightly it hurt. He was holding himself over her, his arms rigid, the veins running through them prominent. "Are you all right?"

Tracey didn't look away. She saw the desire in his eyes, and her heart soared. "Yes, please don't stop," she whispered, her voice ragged.

The intimacy of the act was incredible, binding them together in a way that could only deepen her love. She moved against him, her hips rocking. She knew his control had snapped as he thrust harder, deeper, into her.

Grant's entire body shook as he moved against her, and he called her name in an agony of release. Exhausted, he fell on top of her, his skin covered with a fine layer of moisture.

Tracey held him tight. She didn't dare move. She had no idea of what to do or say. The weight of his body took her breath, though she would gladly have stayed like that forever. It was sheer heaven to be so close to him, to have him inside her. There was still a small spark of desire deep inside her womb. Her heart felt as if it would burst, it was beating so hard and fast.

Grant drew in a ragged breath, and in that moment Tracey felt him emotionally withdraw from her. She caught her own breath as he slowly pulled his body from hers. Her arms tightened around him momentarily, feeling the strain and pull of the hard muscles in his back and shoulders. He was strong and, exerting little effort, easily broke her embrace.

Tracey watched him roll away and sit up on the opposite side of the bed, leaving his back to her. A stark silence fell between them. He leaned over and hung his head in his hands, and his shoulders heaved as he exhaled laboriously.

Staring at his rigid back, Tracey saw him tremble slightly. She had hoped that sex would be good with Grant, that she would in some way fulfill him. A feeling of inadequacy rushed over her.

Unwilling to let him see her pain, she started to roll over, to turn away and hide her face in the fluffy pillows, hoping it would muffle her sobs should she be unable to hold in the agony she felt inside. Grant's hand shot out and gripped her thigh. His fingers bit into her flesh, preventing any movement.

"Don't," he commanded quietly, still not looking at her. "Just give me a couple of minutes." His words came out hoarse, sounding abrasive and torn. Grant felt as if he'd lost a part of himself when he was inside Tracey. He hadn't expected that, hadn't thought she could do that to him. He needed control, needed to keep her in the neat little place he'd made for her in his life.

From somewhere deep inside, Tracey found the courage to speak, though her own voice came out rusty, untried. "It's okay. Sex has never been that great for me," she admitted. "I'm just sorry it wasn't better for you." Despite her brave words, her voice broke.

Grant's head jerked up and around. "What are you talking about?" His voice sounded hard.

Tracey bit her lip, fighting the sting of hot tears. Of all things, she hadn't expected him to be angry. "I've never been overly sexual. I thought maybe it would be different between us. I—" Unable to continue, her voice broke.

Swallowing hard, she squeezed her eyes shut, feeling humiliated beyond words. In desperation she pulled at the comforter to cover herself, but Grant's other hand grasped the coverings and tugged them out of her reach, leaving her naked and vulnerable to his gaze. With a look of desperation she covered her breasts with her arms.

"Is that what you think?" he asked quietly. Her cheeks were flushed, and tears glistened her eyes. Even as he realized how much his sudden remoteness had hurt her, his body tightened and swelled until it throbbed, causing him to curse under his breath. Already he wanted her again.

It wasn't enough that he'd pressured her into this marriage, used his children as a bargaining tool and gained a bed partner in the process. That was despicable enough to make him realize what a selfish bastard he really was.

She was his best friend! That he'd so carelessly taken her without seeing to her own needs embarrassed him. He hadn't even pleased her, and here she was apologizing to him for making him feel more like a man than he'd felt in a lifetime.

"You can't even look at me."

Grant met her hurting gaze. "Oh, Trace, you really are something," he said on a soft sigh, and his gaze gentled as it passed over her.

He lay on his back and pulled her on top of him, gathering her against him, holding her close. Her thigh fell between his legs, against his quickening hardness, and Grant kissed the top of her head and said bluntly, "Honey, feel how I respond to you. That's the way a man feels when he wants a woman."

"You don't have to say that to make me feel better," Tracey protested miserably. With his words he'd as much as said any woman would do.

"I couldn't fake that if I wanted to." As if to convince her, Grant gently grasped her thigh and pulled it tighter against him.

"Then why did you turn away from me?" Tracey asked, hurt seeping into her voice.

His heavy sigh was burdened with repentance. He couldn't tell her how affected he'd been by being inside her, couldn't let her know how very much he'd needed her. He couldn't give that kind of power over him to another woman, not even Tracey. Instead, he admitted to his own inability to satisfy her.

"I wanted to please you, to make it good for you. But, it had been a long time for me, and I wanted you too badly. I'm so sorry, more than I'll ever be able to say."

"It's all right—" Tracey's words were cut off when Grant abruptly rolled over and pinned her beneath him so fast that she lost her breath. When she looked up, his eyes were ice-blue and as hard as pure steel, sending a cold shiver up her spine.

"Don't ever say that again. If you thought you

weren't sexual, then it was Richard's fault, not yours. It won't be the same with us.'' His voice was a hoarse whisper as his hot gaze raked her face.

''I'm not expecting miracles. I just want to make you happy.''

''You already did.'' He made her look at him and grinned wickedly. ''I sort of lost it when you were hot and wild beneath me, pleading with your sultry voice, begging me to ease the ache inside you.'' His hands held her head in a firm grip, and he lowered his mouth and drank from her lips.

''Let's try it again,'' he whispered against her mouth. A fierce need gripped him when she returned the bold caress of his tongue, moaning deep in her throat. He lifted his head when they were both out of breath. ''I couldn't stop once I was in you. I swear I tried, but you moved against me, and I was lost. This time I promise I'll get it right.''

For a long time she simply stared at him, then, as if relieved of some burden, he felt her whole body soften beneath his. Her gaze smoldered with unfulfilled desire. Grant was hard and ready for her and wanted to take her again, wanted to bury himself inside her, lose himself again in her softness. Instead, he lifted his body away from hers and lay beside her.

Propped on one elbow, he leaned over her, intent on bringing her pleasure and showing her how good it could be between them. His mouth and tongue caressed first one nipple, then the other, until she arched her back, silently begging for more.

Caught in a whirlwind, Tracey cried out as Grant took more of her breast into his mouth, sucking hard. His hands ran over her body, learning every inch of her. She reached for him, but Grant captured her hands with one of his own, preventing her from touching him.

He knew he'd go up in flames if she touched him. His only concern was to bring her to a fever pitch, to hear her cry out and beg him for release. His mouth and hands relentlessly tormented her until she was ready for him, and still he didn't take her.

She arched her back, and rolled her hips. Grant's mouth came down on hers, his tongue thrusting in, then withdrawing, mimicking the very act of sex. Her tongue dueled with his, boldly inviting the intimacy he promised, and he groaned into her mouth.

He released her hands, and she gripped his shoulders. Her breasts grazed his chest as he moved over her, and he grunted deep in his throat. Parting her legs, Grant moved his mouth lower and lower, tasting her body, watching her move as he touched her with his tongue.

She cried his name over and over until he eased on top of her. Gritting his teeth, he slowly entered her. She was like wet silk as she enveloped him, and he forced himself to hold a tight rein on his own urgent desire.

He could feel her tenderness as she took the length of him. The tiny, helpless sounds coming from her throat told him she was beyond feeling anything but the erotic pleasure he was giving her. Gently, slowly, he rocked his hips, holding himself above her, taking her nipples in his mouth and nibbling them softly.

Tracey's whole world exploded around her as sensation after sensation soared through her, the force of it so strong that she moved her hips against Grant, and she pulled him down to her. His mouth claimed hers, swallowing the primal sound that escaped her lips as he thrust harder into her, over and over again, reaching his own peak moments later.

When finally their breathing became even, he adjusted the covers over them, then rested on his back, drawing her against him, cupping her bottom possessively with his hand.

Tracey sighed contentedly, her head on Grant's shoulder, her arm draped across his chest. She didn't look at him.

"It's never been like that for me before," she confessed quietly. "Thank you."

Grant's heart plummeted. So he'd made sex good for her, shown her how hot she could be, brought her to ecstasy.

And she was thankful.

He wondered why that bothered him so much.

Nine

Grant awoke to find Tracey still snuggled against him, warm and soft and inviting. Instantly his body responded, and he wanted her as much as, if not more than, the night before.

The thought hit him that making love to her twice a day for the rest of his life wouldn't begin to satisfy his hunger for her. She posed a danger to him that he hadn't thought possible. Enjoying the pleasure of her body had repercussions. He'd have to be extremely careful with his heart.

He kissed her brow, her cheek, then touched his lips to hers. She smiled in her sleep and murmured unintelligible sounds as she squirmed closer. Grant decided the torture of holding her in his arms and not making love to her was his hell to pay.

He'd woken her during the night, and they'd made love again. She would be sore and tender this morning, not nearly ready for what he had in mind. He felt the need to protect her, even from his own physical demands.

Tracey opened her eyes slowly, and she tilted her head upward. She looked at Grant, unsure of what to expect. He was wide-awake and watching her.

Remembering his lovemaking, she went hot all over. She'd given herself to him without holding anything back. In the light of day she couldn't help wondering what he thought of her. Maybe he accepted it as lust, or possibly two people pleasing each other sexually. But Tracey's responses to him were natural because she loved him. Yet there was no way she could tell him so.

"Good morning," she whispered, feeling shy. Her leg was over his, and her stomach was pressed firmly against his hip. He raised her leg, letting it brush against him. Intense heat swept through her, and she spontaneously pressed herself against his hard desire.

Grant pulled her on top of him and held her head with his hands as he kissed her thoroughly. Her breasts were crushed against his chest.

Their kisses grew fever hot. Grant's hands kneaded her buttocks, and arousal, swift and sharp, burned through her. Nearly incoherent, Tracey rocked her hips against his rigid manhood. Grant broke off his kiss and tucked her head against his chest, then softly stroked her spine with his hands.

"You're not ready for where this is leading," he told her. Sliding out from under her, he abruptly climbed from the bed and patted her rear. "Come on, sweetheart, the honeymoon's over. We've got to pick up the girls and head for the airport. Our flight leaves in three hours."

Tracey watched him gather fresh clothes from his suitcase, then disappear into the bathroom, the truth of his words ringing in her ears. Inside she felt something warm and tender fade away into a deep, dark, secret place.

Their small, intimate wedding had been lovely. She would never forget the look in Grant's eyes when he said his vows. It didn't matter that it was a script. He'd promised to love and cherish her, and she hoped in her heart that his promise would one day come true.

However, Grant's words as he left the room made a crater in her heart. She didn't need to be reminded that theirs wasn't a real honeymoon. Sure, he'd made love to her, and each time his body had shuddered with a powerful, all-consuming release. That one thought led to another, much-more-disturbing one.

Grant had admitted to the fact that he'd been celibate a long time. She wouldn't let herself mistake for love what was merely his passion for her body.

Tracey sighed as she got out of bed and pulled on her robe. While Grant finished his shower, she hurriedly repacked their clothing, checking the room for articles strewn here and there.

When Grant came out of the bathroom, she rushed in without looking at him. She told herself she was glad their time alone together was short-lived. Picking up the children and getting on with their everyday lives would help her remember where she stood with him.

Not once during the night had he murmured words of love. And he'd never asked for her to love him. She would have to keep her true feelings hidden well.

* * *

A few hours later they were at the airport. Tracey and her mother waited with the children as Grant and her father checked their luggage and arranged for boarding passes.

After hugs and best wishes from Tracey's parents, Grant, Tracey and the girls boarded the airplane to travel to their new home. Grant had driven both cars down over the past two weeks and had flown back each time so they could make the trip as a family.

By early afternoon they'd arrived in Atlanta. Grant claimed their luggage, then carried it to the car, which he'd parked in the long-term lot.

After settling everyone in the car, they headed toward the house Grant had picked out in Dekalb County. Grant told her a little about the house as they rode along.

When they arrived, Tracey decided that Grant's description of the house hadn't done it justice. It was a sprawling ranch-style house on what Tracey surmised was several acres of wooded land.

At the front door Tracey wondered if Grant would carry her over the threshold. Holding the baby, she watched as he put the key in the lock and opened it. Instead of turning toward her, he walked inside with Stephanie following him.

Tracey felt the shadow of disappointment in her heart, then quickly told herself not to be upset, that it was just a silly tradition. But it was also another reminder that their marriage wasn't traditional, that possibly it never would be.

The house was beautiful. Two bay windows in the large kitchen made it bright and sunny. Tracey fell in love with the room the moment she walked into it.

"Grant, it's absolutely beautiful." She spontaneously hugged him, and he circled his arms around her and kissed her until she was breathless. She gave him a smile when he let her go, and it pleased her to see desire flame in his eyes.

"I wasn't sure what you'd like, but I thought about you when I first saw this house. It has five bedrooms, which will give us a spare, plus one for your workshop," he explained.

There was a living room, dining room and a large family room, all built with lots of windows. Their furniture had been placed, but there were boxes everywhere. When Grant showed her their bedroom, Tracey stopped just inside. She realized the bedroom furniture was new, that it was neither hers nor the set from his house.

"Your bed was too small," Grant explained as he watched her surprised expression.

Tracey looked at the huge king-size bed, then to Grant. "I didn't realize they made beds that big," she teased. She was relieved she wouldn't be sleeping in the same bed Grant had shared with Lisa. At least that reminder of his previous marriage wouldn't be with them.

Grant's sly grin came easily. "Don't worry, I'll be able to find you in it," he said with meaning. He wriggled his eyebrows.

Tracey smiled. "You're sure?" she asked, teasing him back.

"If the girls weren't here, I'd show you." He leaned down and kissed her hungrily.

At that moment Tracey wished the children had been put to sleep for the night.

The rest of their day was full—unpacking boxes

and putting their possessions away, hanging pictures and keeping the kids occupied.

By bedtime the children were worn-out. Tracey had fixed the kids a quick meal, while Grant went out for some takeout for the adults. Stephanie and Kimberly had gone to bed easily, both exhausted from their busy day.

Tracey knew how they felt. She was worn-out herself.

"I don't know how we're ever going to get everything unpacked," she said to Grant when he came into the den carrying two brown bags. She sank into a chair and moaned with pleasure as her muscles relaxed.

"Don't worry, we will. It'll just take some time." He put the bags down and began taking food out. "I found a deli just down the road. Here's your favorite," he announced, handing her a wrapped sandwich.

Tracey removed the paper and took a bite of chicken salad on a soft French roll. "Oh…oh, Grant, this is great," she announced, swallowing and biting again. "What'd you get?" she asked.

He pulled another sandwich from the bag, then handed her a drink before sitting beside her on the sofa. "Roast beef." He unwrapped the sandwich and took a bite. After chewing and swallowing, he said, "It tastes delicious. Although, it could be that I'm just starving."

Tracey shook her head. "No. Mine's to die for. Here, try a bite." She offered her sandwich to him, and he leaned over and helped himself. Some of the juice dripped on her finger, and she stuck it in her mouth to lick it off. She glanced up to find Grant watching her.

There was no mistaking the look of hunger in his eyes; she knew it wasn't for the food. Tracey decided to enjoy the moment. Purposely she slipped her tongue out and licked her finger again, her eyes never leaving his.

"Keep that up," he taunted, "and you're not going to get a chance to finish eating."

"Who's going to stop me?" she asked, slowly running her tongue across her lips.

"Tracey." His blue gaze locked with hers.

"I don't think I'm that hungry anymore," Tracey announced. She put what was left of her sandwich down. She watched Grant put his on the table beside hers. "I think I'll get ready for bed."

She started to get up, but Grant stopped her by grasping her hand. He fell back on the sofa and dragged her down on top of him. Then his mouth was on hers. Tracey moaned when their tongues touched.

She gave herself over to the pleasure of his kisses, thinking she was the luckiest woman on earth. She'd waited forever for Grant to touch her like this. Last night hadn't been enough. She wanted more. She wanted him to make love to her.

Grant's hands found their way up her pink cotton shirt, and Tracey moaned as his fingers slid alongside her breasts. Surely this was heaven, she thought, as she rained kisses on his cheek and along his neck.

Desire consumed her as they both shed their clothing, then came together, sealing flesh against flesh. His palms ran over her buttocks, and she arched her hips.

"Grant." Her breathing was ragged, and she barely managed to get his name out.

Grant's mouth found her breasts, and her cry of pleasure broke the silence of the room.

"I want to be inside you," he rasped. "Now."

Tracey felt him, hard and rigid against her. She edged her body upward, positioned herself, then slid down on him.

Tracey accepted his body into hers, unable to hold back the cry of ecstasy that left her lips. Grant kissed her hungrily as his hips pushed against hers again and again. Fire ripped through them, blazing out of control until they both slipped over the edge.

After a moment Grant got up and went to the bathroom. When he came back, he had a packet in his hand.

"I guess we both forgot," she said quietly.

Grant didn't say anything for a moment. "Don't worry about it," he finally told her, grasping her hand and leading her to the bedroom.

Tracey went into his arms, reminding herself to be more careful in the future.

Grant cast his gaze across the dimly lit banquet hall, taking in the large crowd of people and the party atmosphere. The soft music playing in the background was drowned out by drones of conversations and sporadic laughter. The well-wishers were out in full force, enjoying the opportunity to relax and party, eager to rub elbows with the upper crust of management. It seemed everyone was having a great time.

Grant, however, hated parties. Tonight he hated this one in particular. It made no difference to him that it was being given in his honor, by his own staff, in recognition of his promotion and to welcome him and his family to Atlanta. He *knew* he should be feeling gratitude instead of the resentment that was building to a frustrating level inside him.

He just didn't.

The past three weeks had been hectic to say the least. Grant had worked long hours every day, usually arriving home late in the evening just in time to see his children before their bedtime. He'd promised Tracey he would have more free time soon.

Kimberly seemed to adjust to the changes easily, and Stephanie had stopped sucking her thumb. She was still wheezing from asthma and was under the care of a local specialist. Nearly every day she complained of not feeling well. The problem was she'd become absolutely dependent on Tracey.

Grant knew it was ridiculous, hated even admitting it to himself, but he'd become increasingly jealous of the time his own children spent with Tracey. Stephanie demanded Tracey's attention, and Tracey gave in to the child incessantly. Grant and Tracey had had more than one heated argument over what was best for Stephanie, the latest being right before the party.

Stephanie had begged Tracey to stay home, and Grant had seen by her expression that she'd been about to give in. Well, hell, he'd wanted Tracey with him this evening. Losing his temper, he'd told her to stop pampering Stephanie, that she was his daughter and he knew what was best for her.

Stung by his careless words, Tracey had stared back at him, the hurt in her eyes unmistakable. He'd apologized immediately, but throughout the ride to the party she'd remained quiet, speaking to him only when she had to, ignoring him for the most part.

Stepping away from the bar, Grant searched the room for his wife, then scowled when his gaze landed on her. The ache inside him was becoming all too familiar. He'd never needed anyone the way he needed Tracey. And not just as a mother for his children.

No, Grant had become addicted to her as a woman. He needed her in a basic way. Making love to Tracey was more satisfying than Grant had ever imagined.

Hell, *satisfying* was hardly the word to describe the heights she took him to. He'd never suspected she would respond so wildly to his lovemaking, and sometimes Grant thought he'd go crazy just watching her. She always met him more than halfway, eager to explore and satisfy the fire that burned between them.

But he never forgot for a moment that their marriage was based on friendship rather than love. And he supposed that it was natural, since they didn't love each other, that they would have some rough spots to get through.

He just hadn't expected to feel so attracted to her and so possessive of her. His eyes remained on the group of people with her. It bothered him to see her standing with staff from his office, laughing and smiling, talking easily with them when she'd hardly spoken to him all evening.

Grant's gaze narrowed on the man at Tracey's right. They seemed engrossed in conversation. Tracey's face lit with a warm smile when Dean Garrison leaned over and spoke close to her ear.

It should have pleased him to see how well she was getting along with his staff. It didn't. Grant was surprised by the surge of envy that hit him. Knowing Garrison's penchant for women did nothing to improve his temperament.

Grant had never suspected Tracey could arouse

such intense feelings in him. But then, he'd never expected the sweet, devoted girl he'd known all his life to turn into a vibrant, passionate woman in his bed.

He tensed as he stood watching her. He'd thought that making love to her would have satisfied the lust he'd felt for her before they'd married. Instead, he couldn't seem to get enough of her. Even now his body was on fire from just thinking about taking her home to bed.

Tracey watched as Grant made his way across the room and inserted himself between Garrison and her.

"Grant, old pal, you have a very charming wife." Dean commented, his eyes lingering on Tracey.

When Grant put his arm around Tracey's shoulders in a blatant show of possession, she stiffened slightly, yet he tugged her against his side just the same. "*Wife* is the operative word, Garrison. Go find a woman of your own."

"Grant!" Tracey gasped, and she shot him a warning look. "Mr. Garrison and I were discussing my work. He's interested in having a lamp made as a gift to his parents."

"I see." A muscle flexed in Grant's jaw, revealing the idea didn't exactly sit right with him. "And just when do you think you'll have the time to do it? You were just complaining this morning about how hectic things are, getting Stephanie ready to start school."

"I wasn't complaining," she answered, pinning him with a stare. "I was merely remarking how things would calm down once she starts kindergarten, especially since we now have a part-time housekeeper." Tracey hadn't wanted to take on help, but Grant had

convinced her she would have to if she planned to
get any work done.

She turned back to the other man, her smile sincere.
"I'd love the opportunity to show you some of my
work if you're really interested."

"Oh, I am," he assured her, and he smiled widely.
"And please call me Dean." Reaching inside his suit
jacket, he removed a small leather wallet from the
inside pocket. Flipping it open, he extracted his business card and extended it to her. "Please give me a
call whenever it's convenient for you."

"I'll be happy to." Tracey took the card and
slipped it into her purse. "It was nice meeting you,
Dean."

"My pleasure entirely," he replied.

He excused himself, and a cold silence fell between
Tracey and Grant. Finally, when it was apparent that
Grant wasn't going to apologize, Tracey turned to-
ward him.

"What was *that* all about?"

"I don't like the way you were so friendly with
Garrison." Grant looked around them, then his gaze
went back to Tracey when he was sure they wouldn't
be overheard. His voice was dangerously low. "In my
position the last thing I need to deal with is rumors
about my wife and one of my executives."

"You're being ridiculous," Tracey told him, gritting her teeth.

Grant snorted contemptuously. "Am I? Suppose
word gets out about our marriage. Your behavior with
Garrison, given his reputation with women, would
cause gossip and do irreparable damage to my au-
thority."

If Tracey had the slightest idea that Grant's sudden

possessiveness stemmed from his feelings for her as his wife, she would have been thrilled. However, she knew better. Grant had said or done nothing in the past few weeks to make her feel their marriage was based on more than friendship and his need for her help. And, of course, lust.

"Marrying you did not give you the power to make decisions for me, Grant. You just remember that," she cautioned him. Their marriage was supposed to be a partnership. Those were *his* ground rules. She abided by them, and she expected him to, also.

Grant reached out and cupped the back of Tracey's neck, drawing her closer to him. He bent down to her, his eyes like black stones, their message clear. "I'm warning you, Tracey. Stay away from Garrison. I don't like the way he looks at you."

When they arrived home, Tracey said good-night to their housekeeper and went directly to check on the girls before changing out of her evening clothes and getting ready for bed. She had just pulled her nightgown on and was brushing out her hair when Grant came in from seeing the housekeeper to her car.

Tracey avoided looking directly at him as he approached her and placed his hands on her bare shoulders. They slid possessively down the front of her gown and cupped her breasts. Her eyes went to his in the mirror, and though they stared at each other in taut silence, neither could deny the desire that swept through them.

As Grant's hands began a tormenting, erotic massage of her body, Tracey leaned back against his hard length. He moved his hips and pressed his swollen manhood against her. Despite their earlier arguments, physically they still wanted each other.

Tracey stood and turned, pressing herself close to him, slipping her arms around his neck and lifting her mouth to accept his kiss, never giving thought to refusing him.

She loved him and she would go on loving him. She'd accepted from the start he would never feel the same way. She could no more deny him than she could deny herself.

Grant enjoyed her body thoroughly, branding her his with every single touch of his mouth and hands. Tracey was ready to receive him right away, but he waited until she begged for him to fill her, then took her with a fierce possession that left them both drained.

That evening set the course for the next couple of weeks. Daily, Tracey and Grant went through the motions of their marriage through force of habit. The morning conversations between them were stilted and stressful, adding another burden to their fragile bond of marriage. However, their nights together were far different. No matter how they got along during the day, Grant laid claim to Tracey's body at night, and she went willingly into his arms, wanting whatever he would give of himself.

Tracey was surprised one afternoon when she received a call from Dean Garrison asking once again about her work. They talked for a while, then made plans to get together the next week to talk about a piece for his parents' anniversary. Tracey was thrilled, but hesitated mentioning it to Grant. He'd seemed so distant since they'd moved to Atlanta, and she attributed his remoteness to the strain of his new job.

As luck would have it, she was still so busy settling

in that she forgot about the appointment until one evening when she'd just put the girls to bed and the telephone rang. As usual, Grant was late coming home from work, and Tracey was expecting it to be him. She was surprised when she answered the telephone and it was Dean checking on the time of their appointment.

Tracey told him she was glad he called, repeated the time and gave him directions to the house before hanging up the telephone. She turned when she heard a sound behind her and jumped when she saw Grant. He was standing in the doorway, his shoulder propped against the jamb.

"Who was that?" he asked, his tone suspicious.

"It was, um, Dean…Dean Garrison," she said, using Dean's last name in an effort to make Grant see the man as a client of hers. "He's coming here tomorrow." Her heart raced when she saw irritation flare in Grant's blue eyes.

To Grant's way of thinking, Garrison's name rolled off her tongue too easily. "I told you to stay away from him."

They'd been headed for this argument for days. The strain had been nearly unbearable. Annoyed, she said, "And I told you that you don't own me." She started to move around him, but Grant stepped in front of her, blocking her way.

"You're my wife," he said, his teeth clenched. A muscle worked along his jaw.

"That's right, Grant. I'm your wife, not your possession. You can't order me around, tell me who to see and where to go." Trying to forestall what she could feel coming, Tracey pushed around him and headed for the kitchen. Grant followed on her heels.

"I don't want you seeing Garrison," he repeated. The slam of the bedroom door as he left the room and stalked after her seemed to enforce his demand.

"It's not a date, Grant. I'm going to do some work for him," Tracey explained, reining in her own temper. "And keep your voice down. You'll wake the girls!" she snapped.

"And you weren't going to tell me?" he demanded. "Did you think I wouldn't find out?"

"I wasn't trying to hide it from you," Tracey insisted.

"From your conversation it didn't sound as if this was the first time you discussed it." An accusation was apparent as he waited for her to answer.

Tracey had a feeling she was digging herself a hole. "Okay, it wasn't. He called me last week, and we arranged a date and time. He was calling back tonight to confirm." She waited for Grant to digest her words.

"That's what you call being honest?" Grant asked.

Tracey had wanted him to learn to trust her, but she realized then that her tactical error would be hard to overcome.

"Forget it. I don't want you to see him."

"Why not?" she demanded, not understanding his obsession with the subject of her work. For the past few weeks he'd been like a stranger to her. He'd been withdrawn, keeping himself at a distance from her nearly every waking moment of the day. Well, she'd had enough. "You said you wouldn't mind if I continued working after we married. What's changed?"

"I *don't* mind you working. I told you I don't like the way Garrison looks at you," Grant retorted, then stepped closer to her. "His eyes were all over you at that party. I could have ripped them right out of their sockets.''

Surprised by the vehemence in his tone, Tracey's eyes widened. ''That hardly makes sense. We were talking about my work,'' she insisted as they entered the kitchen.

Grant grunted. ''*You* were talking about work. Garrison had something altogether different on his mind, so just stay the hell away from him. I don't trust him.''

Tracey stood still and let his words sink in. Finally she asked quietly, ''Or is it me you don't trust?'' She watched his reaction, saw him flinch. ''What's happened between us? Why all of a sudden don't you trust me? You know I'd never do anything to hurt you or the girls.''

Grant's eyes narrowed on her, then he swore savagely. Without another word he turned and started from the room. Tracey caught his arm and held on when he would have pushed her away. He didn't look at her, and she spoke his name, her voice pleading. Finally he raised his eyes to hers, and she saw his pain and desperation.

She was stunned. Did he feel threatened?

Ten

Silence fell between them. That was it, Tracey thought. Grant was letting pain eat him up inside, and he was never going to allow her in his heart.

"You can't truly believe I'd be interested in another man." Her eyes narrowed on his face, and she thought for a moment he might possibly be jealous. Could he possibly love her?

"I'm in love with you, Grant," she whispered, looking directly into his eyes. The admission came easily, for she wanted to reassure him and she could no longer hold in her true feelings. "I've always loved you, even when you married Lisa."

Grant groaned and reached for her. He crushed her against him and kissed her hungrily. Tracey met his desire equally and gave herself to him. He swiftly lifted her onto the kitchen table, then nudged her knees apart and stepped between them.

His hands reached for her blouse as his lips hungrily devoured her mouth. Tracey worked fast on the buttons on his dress shirt while he opened her bra and massaged her breasts.

She put her arms around his neck when he came down over her, her hands in his hair, urging his mouth back to hers. He kissed her hard, possessively, and his hands slid beneath her black skirt and pulled her panties off.

Tracey gasped from the abrupt action, her excitement and desire heightened even more when she heard the rasp of the zipper of his trousers.

Then he was inside her, and she couldn't stop the sound of pleasure that escaped her lips. Tracey strained against him and locked her legs around his middle, telling him with her body and heart how much she loved him.

"Tell me again," he demanded, and moved against her with slow, drugging strokes that made them both groan with pleasure. "Tell me!" It came out sounding like a plea.

She raised her lids and met his hot gaze as he continued to thrust into her. "I love you, Grant, so much," she rasped, short of breath. She closed her eyes and moaned deep in her throat as he rocked into her deeper and deeper.

"Trace," he hissed. It was a heady experience, her love, more than he'd ever asked for or expected. Grant wanted to prolong their union, but he couldn't stop his body from responding to her passion.

Knowing she loved him sent him over the edge, and any control he'd had shattered into a million brilliant pieces. He claimed her mouth as she tightened her legs around him and begged him to move faster.

When she climaxed, his world exploded, and he called out her name.

He didn't, couldn't move away from her. He continued to titillate her, slowly moving against her and savoring the electrifying sensations that claimed them. He braced himself on his arms, just high enough to see her face.

"Open your eyes, honey. Look at me." Tracey obeyed, and Grant's heart raced when he saw them glazed with passion. "Please don't ever leave me, Trace. I don't think I could stand it."

He sounded so desperate that Tracey held back tears. He hadn't said he loved her, and her heart broke a little. It all came back to trust. The thought that he still held his heart out of her reach didn't stop her from telling him how she truly felt. "I could never think of leaving you," she whispered. "You're a part of me. You always have been. I'll love you always."

Grant kept her pinned beneath him. He wanted to believe Tracey, but his heart wouldn't let him.

With feelings that bordered on anxiety, he tightened his arms around Tracey. He wanted to tell her how much she meant to him, how much he cared for her. But the words wouldn't come. He knew it was irrational, but his heart had been sorely bruised once, and he didn't want to live through that kind of pain again.

He didn't want to love Tracey. He didn't want her to mean that much to him, to depend on her for survival. As long as she was just his wife, as long as he kept her neatly in that role, he would be in control.

"I think you'd better let me up," Tracey finally said, still quite breathless. "I don't believe they had this in mind when the table was built."

"You'd probably be surprised," Grant answered. "Though I have to admit that I'm never going to be able to sit at this table again without remembering the way you looked when I made love to you on it."

Silence stretched between them as he moved and let Tracey up. After straightening their clothes, they went to bed, where Grant gathered her close to his body.

For the first time in her life Tracey felt cherished. Even though Grant hadn't said the words of love she needed to hear, she had to believe that what they had was strong enough to make their new marriage last. She savored the moment.

Their relationship changed dramatically over the next few weeks, and Tracey expressed her love for Grant by holding nothing back. In response to her openness, Grant was attentive and caring, showing her over and over again how much he desired her. Though their lovemaking before was incredulous, now there was a tenderness between them that brought them closer together.

Grant became devoted to his children and her. He often talked of their future, of what he wanted to accomplish in life, things he wanted to give Tracey, places he wanted to take her.

And he'd changed all his legal papers to list Tracey as his wife. She hadn't realized he thought about those things until he brought it up.

Tracey had been friends with Grant for years and thought there wasn't anything she didn't know about him. She soon found out how wrong she was.

Grant was a closet romantic.

He brought her fresh flowers often and took her out

on ''dates.'' He surprised her with breakfast in bed. He said he didn't want her to feel taken advantage of, that he wanted her to know how much he cared about her. It wasn't an admission of love, but for Tracey it was the next best thing.

For a person who didn't like change, Tracey decided this was a change in her life that was for the better. She was happier than she'd ever been.

On the morning of Thanksgiving, Tracey got up early to begin dinner preparations, but it seemed she had to drag herself out of bed. Her parents had arrived several days before, and each evening they'd all stayed up late talking. She blamed her lethargy on too little sleep and too much to do. By the time she'd prepared the turkey and slid it in the oven, she was feeling markedly better.

After breakfast Helen and Bill took the girls to the neighborhood park to play, and Grant and Tracey used the time to put together the rest of the meal.

When her parents and the children returned, dinner was ready. The next few minutes were filled with sounds of laughter and talking as the food was passed around and plates were filled.

''Everything looks wonderful. I feel guilty for eating when I wasn't here to help you two.'' Helen glanced up at her daughter, but Tracey's expression made her catch her breath.

''Oh!'' Tracey's fork hit her plate with a loud clang, and everyone stopped talking at once. Tracey stared at her food, revulsion widening her eyes. Throwing her hand over her mouth, she came abruptly to her feet. Her chair crashed to the floor as she rushed from the table.

Grant went in search of her and found her in the bathroom bent over the toilet, her head in her hands, violently losing the contents of her stomach.

"Easy, Trace," he whispered, crouching beside her. His hand caressed her back with a slow, circling motion.

"I'm all right," she said, but her voice sounded ragged. Her stomach muscles were pulled taut.

As quickly as the nausea came, it subsided. Tracey moaned and sank back on her heels, then slumped against Grant. He slid his arms beneath her legs, then stood and carried her to the bedroom. Carefully he lowered her to the bed. A frown creased his brow as he stood over her.

"Rest, sweetheart. I'll stay here with you." He sat on the edge of the bed, his eyes never leaving her.

Tracey opened her eyes and met his worried look. "I'm feeling better. I don't know what came over me. Too much excitement, I guess."

"No doubt," Grant murmured, not feeling nearly as sure as he sounded. "Just take it easy. You've been doing way too much." He was worried about her. Her business had really taken off the past few weeks, and she'd been working way too hard. Then there was that rash of viruses making the rounds. He'd had several employees off work with it for the past two weeks.

"I'm all right now," she insisted. She pushed up on her elbows, but that was as far as she got before Grant placed his hand on her shoulder.

"Stay put," he ordered, then touched his lips to her forehead. She wasn't sure if he was checking her temperature or kissing her.

"I'm already feeling better," Tracey persisted.

Grant's look was doubtful. "Well enough to eat?" he asked, darting her a suspicious look.

Tracey fell back on the bed and moaned. "Don't be cruel." A new wave of nausea passed through her.

"That's what I thought. Stay here and rest. I'm going to check on your parents and the girls. I'll be right back."

He left the room, and Tracey curled onto her side, her legs drawn up to her chest. She slowly closed her eyes. She woke up much later, and Grant was sitting on the edge of the bed watching her.

"How long have I been asleep?" she asked lethargically.

"A few hours," Grant answered, running his gaze over her. "How do you feel?" He put a hand to her cheek.

"Better." She swung her legs off the bed and stood up, straightening her badly wrinkled clothes.

"Are you sure?" Grant asked, not quite convinced.

She yawned and covered her mouth with her hand. "Yes. Where are the girls?"

"With your parents in the den."

Assuring Grant she was fine, Tracey went to join her family.

Over the next couple of days, Tracey felt okay in the morning, but by afternoon her energy was zapped and nausea hit her hard.

She was resting on the sofa in the evening when Grant came in late from work. When she opened her eyes, he was kneeling beside her, his expression one of concern.

"You all right?" he asked, gently stroking her cheek with his knuckles.

"Yes, of course," she answered, sounding sleepy rather than ill. "I'm sorry. I guess I drifted off waiting for you."

"Where are the girls?" he asked.

Tracey explained that she'd put them to bed early, admitting that she hadn't felt well earlier.

"This has gone on long enough," Grant said, and there was no patience in his tone.

Feeling much better, Tracey got up and went into his arms, hugging him to her. She turned her face up to his. "I'm feeling fine now."

Grant studied her for a moment. There were faint circles under her eyes, and she looked a little pale. "Tomorrow I want you to see a doctor," he said in a tone that warned her not to argue. "You've been feeling lousy for two days." When she started to protest, he glared at her. "No arguments. And don't use the excuse that you don't know one, or I'll personally take you myself."

"Okay, okay," she finally agreed.

The following morning Tracey went to one of those small emergency care centers that seemed to be on every other corner. The doctor examined her thoroughly, then left the room to check on her test results.

He returned with a smile on his craggy face. "Well, this explains your symptoms," he commented. Then he told her, "You're pregnant."

"Pregnant!" Tracey exclaimed. "That's impossible!"

The silver-haired doctor's amused expression never wavered as he studied his young patient. "I assure you that it's more than possible."

Tracey was adamant. "You don't understand. My husband and I have been pretty careful since we got married.'' They'd used condoms at first, then Tracey had started using a diaphragm. She'd had to talk Grant into letting her handle the birth control, but she had wanted to be as close to him as possible. She told as much to the doctor.

''Pretty careful?'' the doctor repeated.

Tracey blushed. She could think of several occasions that first week or two when they'd been careless, carried away by passion. But they'd been very careful ever since.

Still in a state of disbelief she explained, ''Even in my previous marriage, I tried to have a baby, but wasn't able to get pregnant,'' she explained. The doctor nodded his head as she talked, listening intently to every word. ''So you see, you've made a mistake. I can't be pregnant.''

The doctor merely gave her a patient smile. ''What about your former husband? Was he tested?'' he asked as he fished a pen out of his pocket, then wrote something on her chart.

''Well, no,'' she answered, shaking her head. ''My doctor suggested it, but he wouldn't go.'' Having a child wasn't a priority for Richard, and he'd insisted that they had plenty of time. That had been a bone of contention between them.

''Then the problem could very well have been his,'' the doctor stated. ''No birth control method is 100 percent foolproof, even if you've been pretty careful.'' He smiled wryly. ''Sometimes Mother Nature intervenes. I can assure you, young lady, you are with child. My guess would be about three months along.''

''Three months.'' Tracey did some quick math, calculating the days she and Grant had been married.

"I've only been married a little over three months," she confessed. She'd attributed her missed periods to anxiety and excitement over marriage to Grant and the move to Atlanta.

"It's not unheard of for a woman to get pregnant when she first gets married."

Tracey nodded, wondering how Grant would take the news.

On the ride home she repeatedly told herself she wasn't dreaming. Her heart swelled. She was going to have a child. Her very own baby.

Grant's baby.

Reality swept in like a gale-force wind, and the full impact of her pregnancy hit her as she arrived home. Tracey sat in the car and stared into oblivion.

She relived the night Grant asked her to marry him, as if it were yesterday. He'd told her he never wanted to father another child. Tracey had agreed to this marriage with that knowledge. She'd told Grant she could live without having her own children, that Stephanie and Kimberly would fulfill her role as a mother. At the time it had been the truth.

How was she going to tell Grant about the baby?

Tracey worried about it all afternoon. She put the girls to bed early to give her and Grant some time alone together. They needed to talk. There was much more at stake now, not just their marriage and their family, but a beautiful new life growing inside her.

Tracey hoped Grant would accept the news rationally. She knew it would be a shock to him, just as it was to her, but in her heart she needed to believe he would be happy for her, for them both.

Since she'd confessed her love, he seemed content with their life together, and there was a special bond between them. Though he hadn't said so, Tracey felt he loved her. Why he couldn't say the words, she didn't know.

He'd been young when his mother died. Her death had come so suddenly, and her absence in his life had broken his heart. Then his wife had left him. Those were painful memories to release. Maybe Grant wasn't ready to let Tracey in his heart. But she could wait, and she would love him forever—even if he was never able to tell her he loved her.

It was late when he arrived home, and she met him at the door as he came in from the garage.

"Hi," she said, kissing his cheek, noticing the lines of tension in his face. "You look tired." And unapproachable, she thought. Or was she just looking for an excuse to save her news for later? She took his briefcase and put it aside. "Are you hungry?"

Grant pulled her to him and kissed her, his lips lingering to taste her mouth thoroughly before he pulled away. He frowned when she put her hands against his chest instead of around his neck.

"I kept your dinner warm." She moved out of his arms and opened the oven door. Grant took a seat at the kitchen table, and she put a plate of food in front of him. As he ate, she made him a glass of tea. "How was your day?" she asked, taking a seat across from him.

"Awful. Robert's having problems in Columbia. I was on the telephone with him most of the afternoon," Grant answered, wearily stretching his shoulders. He swallowed the last bite of food, then scooted his chair back and stood. "I'm beat," he said, rubbing his neck. "I need a quick shower and bed."

Tracey nodded. "Sure. Go on up. I'll join you after

I clean this up.'' She gestured at the dishes on the table.

Tracey watched him leave, and dread consumed her. When she got upstairs, she heard Grant in the shower so she changed into her nightgown and got into bed.

Grant hadn't asked her how her doctor's appointment had gone, and she was glad. Apparently his day had been so busy that he'd forgotten she was going. She didn't want to put off telling him about the baby, but it was important to her to wait until the right time. She didn't want to tell him when he was tired and exhausted. She decided to talk to him in the morning.

Though Grant had been tired when he came home, it seemed he'd found a spark of energy when he climbed into bed. He pulled her in his arms and began to touch her body intimately, and Tracey melted against him.

His lovemaking that night was tender and fulfilling, and Tracey relished every pleasurable moment with him. Knowing she was carrying his child made the intimacy they shared even more special to her. They fell asleep in each other's arms.

Tracey hadn't planned on waking and finding that Grant had already left for work. For several days it seemed there just wasn't time to have a private talk. Between Tracey's work and Grant's job and the girls preoccupying their evenings, Tracey hadn't had a chance to talk with Grant about her news.

Things between them had been so comfortable that she just didn't want to rock the boat. She hoped she was being silly, but apprehension filled her every time she tried to broach the subject. It was just easier not saying anything. She finally got up enough courage to approach him one morning before he went to work.

As he came out of the bathroom, Grant looked at Tracey, who was standing beside her dresser. He started to dress, pulling on his trousers and buttoning his blue shirt. He was so attuned to her moods he asked, ''What's wrong?''

Tracey clasped her shaking hands together behind her back. ''We need to talk.''

''Sounds serious.'' Frowning, Grant pulled on his shoes and socks, then went to the closet to select a tie to go with the dark-blue suit he was wearing. He ran his gaze over Tracey. She was still in her nightgown and white robe. Just looking at her made him want her.

''That depends on how you're going to accept what I have to tell you.''

Grant's gaze connected with Tracey's, and for the first time he saw real fear in her eyes. ''I'm listening,'' he answered, giving her his full attention.

''I had a doctor's appointment last week.''

His expression contrite, Grant approached her. ''I'm sorry I didn't remember,'' he apologized. ''Why didn't you tell me about it?'' Grant studied her closely and saw how upset she was. His stomach turned to lead. He knew she hadn't been feeling well, had insisted on her going to the doctor. He couldn't believe he'd forgotten to ask her about it.

Trying to quell the panic rising inside him, Grant walked over to her. When he started to touch her, she back away from him. ''Trace, honey, what is it?''

''I'm pregnant,'' she blurted out. Her body tensed, and her teeth sank into her bottom lip.

Grant stopped in the process of reaching for her. "What?"

"I'm pregnant, Grant." She saw the look of doubt in his eyes, and her heart lurched.

"You can't be," he replied emphatically, as if saying the words made it so.

"I know how you're feeling. I felt the same way when I found out, but it's true," she insisted, seeing he still didn't believe her.

"A doctor told you this? You had a pregnancy test?" he questioned.

"Yes. I'm going to have your baby." At that moment Tracey saw Grant's whole demeanor change. He no longer looked concerned for her. His hands clenched, and his shoulders visibly tensed. Chills of fear raced down her spine. She'd expected the news of her pregnancy to surprise him momentarily but her hope that he would really be glad for her was quickly washed away by his icy bearing.

"You can't be pregnant," he stated, then he turned away from her. It was quite obvious that he was in denial, that he didn't want to believe it.

"That was my reaction, also," she said cautiously. "I told the doctor about how Richard and I had tried to have a baby. He said the problem must have been Richard. You know, he never would go in for tests." When Grant said nothing, she added, "That's why I was sick. Instead of morning sickness, it hits me in the afternoon."

He looked disconcerted. "But we used protection."

"There were a few times we didn't," she answered, her voice shaking.

He flushed with the reminder. "How far along are you?" he asked, still not looking at her.

"About three months."

Grant tried to quell the terror gripping him. He stared right through her as he slowly digested her words. "Your doctor appointment was over a week ago," he stated, making it sound like an accusation. "Why are you just now telling me? Why didn't you say something when you found out?" he demanded.

"I wanted to," Tracey insisted.

"But you didn't." Grant couldn't help but wonder what else she'd kept from him. It hadn't been so long ago that he'd found out she'd been talking to Garrison. He had started thinking he could trust her. Apparently he was wrong.

Tracey took a deep breath. "No, I—" She put a protective hand to her belly. "I tried to, several times."

Grant couldn't think straight. He wasn't even sure of what to say to her. He only knew that he couldn't stand the thought of her not being honest with him. "Tracey, you knew how I felt when we got married."

Tracey's face turned ashen. "This is your baby, Grant. Yours and mine—" Her voice broke and she caught her breath.

Grant paced the room and then turned to face her, his expression bleak. "I can't believe this is happening," he stated harshly. Pain, sharp and debilitating, whipped through him. She was cutting his heart open, ripping him apart.

She tricked you. The words exploded in his mind, blocking all rational thought. *She lied to you before about Garrison,* a little voice taunted.

"Did you plan this all along?" The mistrust in his tone was unmistakable.

Tracey winced. "Of course not!"

"You said you loved me. What else have you lied about?" he demanded.

"I do love you. I've never lied to you."

"What about Garrison?" He took a step toward her, then stopped himself. He wanted to touch her, hold her, never let her go. But he couldn't bring himself to do it. He'd trusted her, trusted what they had together. Now she was betraying him.

"I explained about that," she insisted, her voice even. Tracey tried to reason with him. "Grant, listen to me. I love you. I would never deliberately do anything to hurt you." Tears stung her eyes.

"You also said you'd be happy raising my children, not having children of your own. It's pretty obvious to me that you're happy about this."

"How could I not be happy?" she demanded. "This is your baby—"

The telephone rang, interrupting their heated discussion. Tracey automatically reached for it, snatching it up. She spoke into the receiver for a moment, then handed Grant the telephone.

"It's your secretary," she told him, searching his expression.

Grant's gaze pierced her as he took the phone from her. His responses were short and curt, his tone low as he spoke. When he hung up, he walked over to the dresser and pulled out some clothes.

Without speaking, he put on the sports coat to his suit. He then went into the walk-in closet and came out with a suitcase and a garment bag.

"What are you doing?" Tracey asked. Confused, she watched him jam his clothes in the suitcase.

"Robert's called an emergency meeting. I have to fly to Columbia," he stated, his tone flat as he pulled on shoes and socks. "I'm scheduled for a flight that leaves in an hour." He went into the bathroom and came back with his shaving kit. After putting a couple of suits and shirts into the garment bag, he zipped it shut, then did the same to his suitcase.

"You're leaving?" Tracey asked. "Now?"

Taking a deep breath, he sighed. "Maybe this is a good thing. I need time to think. Time away from you." He turned his back on her and grabbed the cases. "I'm booked in the usual hotel. You have the number."

He started for the door, and Tracey stepped in his path. "Please, Grant. Please don't go. Let's talk about this."

Grant's look was hard. "Talk about it? Shouldn't we have talked about it a week ago?" He moved around her and went out the door.

Tracey caught up with him at the back door. Grant turned and gave her a long look. "What do you want me to say, Tracey?" he demanded. "You want me to be happy? Well, I can't be. I thought you were satisfied raising my children, now I find out you're not. What am I supposed to feel? You tell me." He walked away from her.

"I don't want you to leave, Grant!" she persisted. "I love you."

He turned and looked at her, skepticism in his expression. "You have a strange way of showing it." He didn't give her time to answer. Instead he walked out of the house. Stunned, Tracey watched him leave.

When the telephone rang later that night, Tracey raced to it. She heard Grant's voice, and relief quickly gave way to heartache when his tone implied he hadn't come to terms with her love or her pregnancy.

Though he asked how she was, he was distant, as if he'd shut his emotions off. He gave her no clue as to what he was thinking.

She missed him terribly. In her heart she knew he was hurting, that he hadn't meant what he'd said. But she couldn't seem to forget that he'd married her only because she'd been a solution to his problems, not for love.

In the short amount of time they'd been married, Tracey had hoped he would eventually come to love her and that his feelings for her would be strong enough to weather any problems they had to face.

Tracey loved him. She always would.

Was she going to lose him now?

Eleven

Grant walked into his hotel suite, his shoulders sagging and his steps slow. He'd never felt as alone as he had the past two days, and he was glad the meetings in Columbia were over.

He tossed his briefcase in a chair as he tugged his tie loose, leaving it hanging around his neck. He moved to the bed and sat on the edge, then leaned over and held his head in his hands. He remembered little of what had been decided in the meeting. All he'd been able to think about was Tracey.

Pregnant.

A jumble of emotions consumed him. Tracey had deceived him. She'd been the one to talk him out of using condoms after they were married, insisting that she didn't mind using a diaphragm. Had she been more careful, there wouldn't be a baby, and everything would be back the way it was. She'd known how he felt. Had she deliberately tried to get pregnant?

She wouldn't do that. She loves you.

Grant snorted as he laid back on the bed. He'd thought he could trust her. But she'd lied to him before about Garrison, hadn't she?

Because of your jealousy.

Grant admitted to himself that he hadn't been very receptive of Tracey working with Garrison. Perhaps that's why she'd been reluctant to talk about selling a piece of her work to him. Could he really blame her?

Grant felt as if his world had caved in. Tracey couldn't love him and put him through this. He'd told her he didn't want another child. He'd blindly given her the control of protection when he shouldn't have. He'd assumed that she'd be careful and wouldn't get pregnant. If Tracey truly cared for him, if she loved him as she'd said, she'd never have let this happen.

Three months. They'd only been married just over three months, he thought.

Grant suddenly realized that he was as much at fault as Tracey, that she must have gotten pregnant when *he* was the one taking care of birth control. There were times when he hadn't used protection, telling himself that she wouldn't get pregnant, relying on the fact that she hadn't gotten pregnant before.

Okay, so she was pregnant. Now what? he asked himself mentally. Where did they go from here? Obviously Tracey was happy about her pregnancy. She'd always wanted a child—now she was having one.

His.

Grant knew how selfish it was of him to have expected her to be happy raising his children and giving up the dream of having her own child.

He was the one with the problem, he decided.

By keeping her at a distance, he was the one who had built the wall between them, the wall that kept him safe from hurt. But it hadn't really worked, had it?

Because he *was* hurting.

Had he lost Tracey by not loving her?

Losing Tracey would kill him, Grant told himself. He didn't think he could stand the sudden terror gripping his heart. He rubbed at his eyes with his hands, feeling the moisture that collected in them.

Losing Tracey would kill him.

The thought reverberated through his mind, tugging at the corners, making him face his innermost feelings. From the moment Tracey had said she was pregnant, Grant had refused to let himself believe the truth. It wasn't really that he didn't trust her. He'd trusted her with his children. He'd trusted her enough to marry her.

He'd trusted her with his love.

He loved Tracey, and that scared him to death.

Grant had no idea of when he'd opened his heart and let Tracey's love in. It wasn't something new that he'd discovered once he'd married her, though marriage to her had deepened his feelings. No, Grant knew his love for Tracey had always been there, just beneath the surface, hidden like a pearl in an oyster shell, waiting to be discovered. He and Tracey were meant to be together.

There was so much about Tracey that he loved. He'd thought he'd known her inside and out, but he hadn't. She was completely unselfish and caring;

she'd taught Grant the true meaning of sacrifice and love. If they gave awards for dedication, she would take the top honor.

He'd thought that his job as vice president was what would make him happy. But in her slow, patient way, she'd shown him that true happiness came from inside.

It wasn't her fault that he was a slow learner, he thought wryly.

Grant loved her, and that was what mattered. A weight lifted from his shoulders. God, he'd been so stupid. Instead of feeling sorry for himself, he should have considered Tracey's feelings. He should have been happy for her. *And he was happy,* he realized, a smile forming on his face.

Tracey was having his baby!

Getting up from the bed, Grant hurriedly packed his belongings. He had to get back to Tracey and ask her forgiveness. She would have to listen to him. She loved him.

At least she had before he'd walked out on her.

When Grant entered his house, it was well past midnight. He'd caught the first flight he could get out of Columbia. Once his plane had landed, he'd wasted no time in getting home. The house was quiet as he tossed his keys on the counter in the kitchen and proceeded through the room. He found Tracey asleep on the sofa in the den, curled in a ball, her knees practically up to her chest.

Her blue leggings contoured her soft curves and her gray T-shirt was bunched around her waist. It didn't take a genius to see that she'd been crying. Rivulets of salt stained her cheeks. Tissues dotted the sofa and carpet around her. Grant felt a tug on his heart. He didn't deserve her forgiveness, but he was going to beg for it.

He quietly walked over to her and knelt beside her. Reaching out, he started to touch her, then stopped, not wanting to startle her. Instead, he softly called her name, then watched as she stirred in her sleep. After a moment she slowly opened her eyes. He'd never seen her so unhappy, and to know that he'd caused her such pain made his heart ache.

"Grant." Wary eyes stared up at him.

Grant started to touch her, but she drew away from him. He realized that he'd done great harm to their relationship. Grant prayed that the damage wasn't irreparable. With remorse that made his heart pound, he let his hand fall to the sofa.

"Trace." His voice cracked a little when he said her name. He saw emptiness in her eyes, hated that he'd been the one to hurt her.

"What are you doing here?" she asked. Her voice was hoarse, her tone quiet, unsure. Her gaze met his with apprehension. She blinked and he saw fresh tears pool in her brown eyes before she glanced away.

"I did a lot of thinking while I was gone. I came back as soon as I could get a flight." He waited a moment, hoping she would look at him. When she didn't, he called her name again. Their gazes collided and his heart jammed in his throat.

"Trace, honey, I'm so sorry that I hurt you," he whispered. The need to touch her was unbearable, yet Grant held back from reaching for her. He'd given up that right, and he had to earn it back.

Tracey slowly sat up. She looked at him again, and her gaze was mistrustful. Grant understood that. The distance between them was more than space, and Grant knew he owed her more than words. He owed her his heart. He only hoped what he had to tell her would be enough to convince her to stay with him, to give him another chance. He wanted to be able to show her how much he loved her.

"I didn't mean the things I said to you," he began, hoping she'd listen to him. "When you told me about the baby, I went a little crazy. I was thinking only about myself, not about you or your feelings. I know you'd never hurt me. I know that," he admitted sorrowfully.

"Do you?" she asked, and her voice broke as her gaze slid away. Fresh tears slipped from her eyes.

Grant could no more stop himself from touching her than he could stop breathing. His hand stroked her hair, her cheek, then rested there. He felt the tremble that went through her.

"In some warped way, I told myself that I couldn't trust you. I thought that your being pregnant meant that you'd let me down. But what I didn't realize was that I was the one letting you down," he admitted. "I thought if I kept you at a distance, I wouldn't get hurt. I didn't realize how much I was hurting you. Trace, I love you."

"Grant, you don't have to say that," she told him. "I'm not going anywhere. I've told you many times that I love you, and I'll never walk away from what we have together."

She didn't believe him. Well, Grant guessed he deserved that. He'd been a stubborn fool. He had to convince her he meant what he'd said.

"I don't blame you for not believing me, but I do love you. I only hope you still love me."

A fragile smile formed on her lips. "How could I not love you? I've loved you since I've known you. Grant, I'm afraid of losing you, losing what we have together," she choked out.

"Hush, babe. I'm the one who's sorry. I've caused you a lot of pain. I didn't think. I was so blinded by my own fears, my own insecurities," he confessed. Grant drew her toward him and into his arms as he sat beside her on the sofa. His lips touched hers briefly. There was so much to say, so much to account for. "I'm so sorry, more than I can ever say. I love you, Trace. Please say you'll forgive me."

Tracey held him to her for a moment, letting herself sink against him, savoring the feel of his arms around her. Then she pulled back and looked deeply into his eyes. "Oh, my, Grant. You do love me," she whispered.

Grant let out a breath when he realized she finally believed him. "I've loved you for a long time. I just didn't let myself accept it."

"What about the baby?" she asked, and for a moment time stood still.

Grant let out the breath he'd been holding. His heart felt as if it was about to explode, and there was pride in his expression. "I'm happy I'm the one who gave you a child." He smiled at her, and the tender look in his eyes proved just how much he meant the words. Then he took her lips with his. His hand slipped behind her head, caressing her neck, pinning her mouth against his own. Finally he lifted his head and stared into her eyes.

"It took the miracle of having a baby together to show me just how much I love you. I almost lost what we have together because I was so afraid of getting hurt. You've taught me how to love again, and I promise you I love our child already.'' His hand went to her belly and rested there.

"It nearly killed me being away from you these past two days," he whispered as he crushed her to him. Grant kissed her lips hungrily, then wiped away her tears. "I've been needing your love all my life, honey. I'll always love you."

Tracey felt tears trail down her cheeks, but she was so happy, she didn't care. "I love you, Grant. So much. Please don't ever leave me again."

Tracey had everything she'd ever wanted in her life: she was a mother, loving Grant's two little girls as if she'd given birth to them; she was going to have a baby, something she'd ached for and never dreamed would happen to her; and Grant loved her.

Life was so good.

Epilogue

Tracey smiled as she and her mother set the table for dinner. "I'm so glad you and dad could visit us for the coming week, Mom." She pressed a hand to her back and rested it there for a moment.

Helen didn't miss the movement, or the way her daughter caught her breath. "We're thrilled to be here for a few days," she said, then she looked a little more closely at Tracey. "Are you all right?" she asked, concern making her frown a bit as she folded linen napkins and laid them beside the plates.

"Yeah." Tracey gave her mother a reassuring smile. "Just tired of being pregnant," she murmured, moving awkwardly around a dining room chair. She put the forks in place, then the knives and spoons.

"I heard that," Grant said, walking into the room with Bill and the girls. They settled the children at the table. "I never thought the day would come when you'd say such a thing.'' He rounded the table and kissed Tracey on the mouth a little too long to be called brief.

"Me, neither,'' she admitted, turning crimson.

"It's not unusual for the first baby to be a little late,'' Helen commented.

Tracey groaned. "I didn't need to hear that, Mom.'' She grinned. "I feel like I'm a balloon about ready to pop.''

Helen poured tea in ice-filled glasses. "Have you two decided on a name yet?''

Tracey's mother had been asking her the same question for months. "Michael if it's a boy and Laura if it's a girl.'' She started to take a seat at the table. "Oh!''

Grant's gaze went immediately to his wife. "What is it? Are you okay?'' he asked, his tone urgent.

"I don't know,'' Tracey admitted, looking worried and in pain at the same time. "I've been having small cramps all day,'' she admitted, realizing now they were getting stronger.

"Why didn't you say something?'' Helen asked, helping Tracey into a chair.

"I didn't want to get everyone excited over nothing.'' She looked at Grant, her expression one of stunned surprise. "I think I'm in labor,'' she declared.

Grant swallowed hard. "You're having the baby? Now?''

"Goodness!'' Helen exclaimed.

"Not right this minute,'' she assured her husband, shaking her head, but enjoying his disconcerted look. "But I think it'll be today.''

"Now everyone calm down,'' Bill said steadily. "Tracey, honey, have you timed the pains?''

Tracey shook her head as another contraction began as a slow ache, building in intensity. She groaned and tried to get up. Grant was by her side immediately. "They just started getting worse," she told her father. As she stood, Tracey was aware that her legs were wet. "My water broke," she declared. "Grant, my water broke," she said again, as if she couldn't believe it.

"Come on, I'll get you to the hospital. Mom, Bill, could you call the doctor and have him meet us there?" Tracey started to walk, but Grant quickly stopped her by sweeping her into his arms and heading for the door.

Bill opened the door, then went out to the garage and helped Grant get Tracey seated comfortably.

"Don't worry about the girls. We'll take care of them."

"Thanks," Grant said. He started the car and backed out, then sped the car forward.

"Grant, honey, we have plenty of time," Tracey said, then caught her breath as a sharp pain grabbed her.

Grant reached for her hand and held it in his. "I'm not taking any chances," he told her. "Just hold on. We'll be at the hospital in no time."

Fifteen minutes later they were at the hospital. The staff of the emergency room knew exactly what to do. Before he knew it, Grant was being ushered into a birthing room with Tracey. They'd gone to classes on having the baby, but the experience was going to be a new one for Grant. He hadn't been in the delivery room when his other children had been born.

Everything passed through Grant's mind like a blur

from that point. Grant coached Tracey on breathing techniques and bathed her face with a washcloth.

Moments later Tracey's doctor, Dr. Jessup, arrived. "I hear you're ready to have this baby," he said by way of a greeting. "I was already at the hospital when I got the message." He checked Tracey over thoroughly. "It won't be too long now," Dr. Jessup said gently to Tracey, patting her hand, then leaving the room.

In fact, it wasn't. Barely an hour went by when Tracey asked Grant to get the nurse attending her. "The baby's coming," Tracey announced, her breathing constricted. "I can feel it." She took a deep breath.

Grant gripped her hand harder. "Hold on, babe."

"I'll try," she said, gritting her teeth. "Hurry," she pleaded as he left the room.

The nurse came back into the room with Grant, checked Tracey, then left again quickly. The next thing they knew, Dr. Jessup came rushing in.

Moments later their son was born. Baby Michael came into the world letting out a soft wail. The nurse wrapped him immediately in a warm blanket and handed him to his father.

"He's beautiful," Grant said, and shared his precious bundle with his wife.

"Oh, Grant, a boy," Tracey answered, her tone full of awe. They had decided early on not to find out the sex of the baby. But over the course of her pregnancy, Tracey had formed a suspicion that Grant would like a son.

Grant gazed in wonder at the tiny squirming infant. "I can't believe we have a son." Turning his gaze on Tracey, he whispered, "I love you so much."

Tracey tried really hard not to cry, but she couldn't help it. She looked from her beautiful baby to her loving husband. "I love you, too. You're the best thing that's ever happened in my life."

Grant leaned closer and kissed his wife. Tracey kissed him back, then held her son for the first time.

How appropriate that her baby had chosen to come into the world today.

It was Mother's Day.

*   *   *   *   *

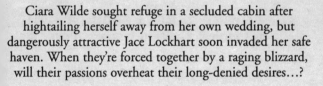
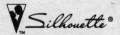

Desire

These women are about to find out what happens
when they are forced to wed the men of their dreams
in **Silhouette Desire's** new series promotion:

The Bridal Bid

Look for
the bidding to begin
in **December 1999** with:

GOING...GOING...WED! (SD #1265)
by **Amy J. Fetzer**

And look for
THE COWBOY TAKES A BRIDE (SD#1271)
by **Cathleen Galitz** in **January 2000:**

Don't miss the next book in this series,
MARRIAGE FOR SALE (SD #1284)
by **Carol Devine,** coming in **April 2000.**

The Bridal Bid only from **Silhouette Desire.**

Available at your favorite retail outlet.

Where love comes alive™

Don't miss Silhouette's newest cross-line promotion,

Four royal sisters find their own Prince Charmings as they embark on separate journeys to find their missing brother, the Crown Prince!

The search begins in October 1999 and continues through February 2000:

On sale October 1999: **A ROYAL BABY ON THE WAY** by award-winning author **Susan Mallery** (Special Edition)

On sale November 1999: **UNDERCOVER PRINCESS** by bestselling author **Suzanne Brockmann** (Intimate Moments)

On sale December 1999: **THE PRINCESS'S WHITE KNIGHT** by popular author **Carla Cassidy** (Romance)

On sale January 2000: **THE PREGNANT PRINCESS** by rising star **Anne Marie Winston** (Desire)

On sale February 2000: **MAN...MERCENARY...MONARCH** by top-notch talent **Joan Elliott Pickart** (Special Edition)

ROYALLY WED
Only in—
SILHOUETTE BOOKS

Available at your favorite retail outlet.

Visit us at www.romance.net

SSERW

**Start celebrating Silhouette's 20th anniversary
with these 4 special titles by
New York Times bestselling authors**

Fire and Rain*
by Elizabeth Lowell

King of the Castle
by Heather Graham Pozzessere

State Secrets*
by Linda Lael Miller

Paint Me Rainbows*
by Fern Michaels

On sale in December 1999

Available at your favorite retail outlet
*Also available on audio from Brilliance.

Where love comes alive™